CHAPTER ONE

When Lissa Massey closed the weathered Blue Vale schoolhouse door, she glanced at her widowed mother's dusty Model A parked along the rusty wire fence. "Oh, no. Not Aunt Gustie tonight," she mumbled.

Lean, stony-faced Aunt Gustie waved her crochet-edged handkerchief as she peered out the right window of the Ford parked between the leaning fence and the ragged sumac bushes.

"Evening, Aunt Gustie," Lissa said. She yanked open the driver's door and tossed her imitation leather satchel in on the striped cloth-covered back seat.

"Evening, Niece. My, ain't it a hot evenin? I bummed a ride back from Lit Watson's store with Melvin Pempton in one of his used tin Lizzies. Bought me a can of salmon and soda crackers at the store." Aunt Gustie's face split into a self-satisfied grin.

Lissa hoped Aunt Gustie didn't think she was a burden. It was just the weariness causing Lissa's shoulders to droop after wrangling with the sixteen pupils at Blue Vale, corralling and cajoling them to settle down and focus their brains on their *Strayer Upton* arithmetic books and *Elson Grey* readers in such heat.

Lissa knew Aunt Gustie, living alone in her three-room cabin, overgrown with trumpet vine on the banks of Dodie Creek, had a heart mellowed to a golden goodness by the upshots and valleys of her life. Only a flooded Dodie Creek would keep her from a Wednesday night supper at the Massey table.

On the western horizon a turquoise cloud with a black underbelly boiled in the sudden upshot of wind. Thunder rumbled. The little Ford shook.

"Big black cloud yonder toward Four Crossing." Aunt Gustie peered out the window, eyes bulging, wrinkles on her forehead matching the ripples in the washboard lane. "Respectable rain over at Lit Watson's store. Better get this high-powered Lizzie across Dodie Creek before the water rolls over the ford." She stroked the wart on her bony chin.

They rocked down the rutted lane leading to the gravel road as Lissa tried to keep in mind her mother's words, "Be patient with her, Lissa, Aunt Gustie's like a lizard plastered in the sun too long, she needs a shady and restful place."

So Lissa remembered that patience was a virtue, according to Preacher Supple over at White Oak Church, east by the burr oaks on the shady banks of Dodie Creek. He admonished the country folk on Christian living as if he were unrolling a never ending scroll.

Lissa steered the gunmetal-colored Model A down the road past the plum thicket. Brother Supple was right. Her mind wandered as she thought of how much longer he would have the strength to preach for them. Surprised them one Sunday by having hollow-cheeked, dark-eyed Brandon Fall "try out" by giving them a sermon.

"Better'n 'em old-timers," the church folks said. Lissa wasn't surprised. She'd always known Brandon Fall as a serious thinker, buying Old Testament history and worn New Testament commentaries from used book stores up in Springfield, poring over them by lamplight.

Since then Brandon, who some folks believed looked like Abraham Lincoln, had been preaching once a month. She wished his suit wasn't so threadbare, pinching his shoulders and hanging like an old gunny sack on his frame. She smiled, remembering how the ceiling seemed to lower when he stood behind the old plank pulpit. Some folks thought Brandon was shy, but you could hear his reverberating voice on the back bench, that is, if the women weren't making too much noise with those Blessed Rest Funeral Home pasteboard fans.

Lissa's mind wandered as Aunt Gustie hunched in her seat and

A Branson Love

An Ozark Romance

by
James D. Yoder

PublishAmerica
Baltimore

© 2002 by James D. Yoder.

All rights reserved. No part of this book may be reproduced in any form without written permission from the publishers, except by a reviewer who may quote brief passages in a review to be printed in a newspaper or magazine.

This novel is a work of fiction. Any references to real people and places are used only to give a sense of reality. All of the characters are the product of the author's imagination, as are their thoughts, actions, motivations, or dialogue. Any resemblance to real people and events is purely coincidental.

First printing

Cover painting by Susan Bartel

ISBN: 1-59286-132-6
PUBLISHED BY PUBLISHAMERICA BOOK PUBLISHERS
www.publishamerica.com
Baltimore

Printed in the United States of America

To all who love the hills and Ozark Mountains of Missouri and Arkansas

Rejoice in the Lord alway: and again I say, Rejoice. Let your moderation be known unto all men. The Lord is at hand.
– Philippians 4:4-5

peered over the wind-blighted countryside where the corn leaves rattled like starched ribbons. Brown heads of coneflower and broken sunflowers raked the hot air. No, Brandon doesn't look like Abraham Lincoln to me. Eyes sad as Lit Watson's beagle, but who wouldn't have sad eyes, scraping sandrocks on that forty acres, calling it farming? Lissa knew Brandon's mind was focused on going to seminary some day.

Once President Roosevelt brought this great old U. S. A. around from the brink of the Depression, Brandon would get on with his Bible studies. Lissa knew it. She hoped he wouldn't cave in and join the Civilian Conservation Corps President Roosevelt set up to provide work for the starved-faced young men leaning on porches and hickory trees waiting for work, just as the cracked land waited for rain.

Lissa wished Aunt Gustie wouldn't tease her about marrying, now that she was twenty. Lissa knew that would have to be postponed with the drought, the bank closings, and the money her mother owed on the farm at the Branson Citizen's Bank.

The car lurched over a sandrock as Lissa turned to enter the half-mile-long stretch where the sycamores overshadowed the ochre road by the east bank of Dodie Creek.

"Look at the way them grasshoppers et up that corn, what survived the dry weather." Aunt Gustie's sun-spotted hand with its berry-stained fingernails stroked her inverted pyramid chin. "These got to be the worst times since them bushwhacker and Bleeding Kansas days."

"Hard times, Aunt Gustie, hard times. I'm thankful for my teaching job."

"Well, that's another matter, ain't it?" Aunt Gustie chuckled and turned her road map face toward Lissa.

Lissa had tried to follow Preacher Supple's admonition about humility and not gloat over the fact that she was a schoolteacher with twenty college hours and a teaching certificate to her credit. Well, so was Marla Edith Maggler a teacher. That was another matter, Marla Edith turning thirty, lying about her age.

Lissa checked her tightly pinned hair with her tanned hand, glad her blond hair had stayed up all day in spite of the fact that she had raced across the schoolyard playing King of the Mountain with the students during recess.

The cloud with the turquoise bottom loomed closer. "Better step on the gas, raining over yonder." Aunt Gustie's glassy eyes shifted as she stared at Lissa's hair. "You ain't gonna get one of them ugly bobs, are you, Lissa?" Aunt Gustie sealed her wrinkle-etched lips above her jutting chin and focused her gravel eyes at Lissa.

"No, not yet," Lissa said, eyes narrowing as she noticed the cloudbank darken in the west. She thought of Marla Edith Maggler's short bob. "Cicily Woodburne styled Marla Edith's hair," Lissa said.

"Well, coarse hair don't bob good," Aunt Gustie continued. "Can't saw off a horse's tail with a butcher knife and 'spect it to look like anything." Her eyes took on the look of an old hen surveying a dried toad.

"Why, Aunt Gustie, I think Marla Edith's hair looks fine." Lissa knew that if she ever bobbed her hair, Aunt Gustie would unload on her. Her fine-textured hair fell in wavelets, she knew it would easily take a curl, and not a spit curl like Marla Edith's, which stuck on her forehead like a black question mark.

"Question mark and questionable character," Aunt Gustie simpered, freckled elbow jiggling on the thin window ledge.

Lissa knew her old aunt was referring to the way Marla Edith's flesh strained the seams of her sleeveless black rayon dress. Sported high heels, too. She knew the men who sat on the whittling bench in front of Watson's store boasted that Miss Marla Edith was about the only woman in Taney County who really knew how to walk in high heels.

Wouldn't want the stubble-faced old codgers on that sagging plank, emptying their mouths of their cud and saying such things about me, pondered Lissa. "Aunt Gustie, it's pouring down over west. Blessing if it'd reach here, even though it's too late to help the crops." Lissa gripped the wheel as the wind whipped the Ford. Up ahead the brown grasses parted, and a tall, thin young man, dragging his patched shirt in one hand, sauntered to the road edge by the stand of persimmon, broad, bony shoulders bared to the wind.

"Well, I'll swan, what's Brandon Fall doing dragging across the road this time of the evenin?" Aunt Gustie muttered.

A BRANSON LOVE

Lissa let up on the gas pedal. Should she stop and chat?

Lissa knew Aunt Gustie'd rail at her if she stopped to pass the time with a bare-chested man, dragging his shirt in one hand, let alone having him lean in your car window, batting those long dark eyelashes at you, sweat dripping from his brow beneath that curly brown hair.

Lissa could see Brandon had spied them and was attempting to slip his shirt over his sweaty back, struggling to get it buttoned. Her shoe pressed the brake pedal, and the Ford rocked to a stop before Brandon had his shirt buttoned all the way up. Lissa smiled, nervous at the chance encounter. Her cheeks blushed in the heat, but it wouldn't be right, not stopping and being neighborly. After all, hadn't Brandon Fall escorted her to evening services half a dozen times already?

Brandon placed a work brogue on the dusty running board and leaned toward her, brown curls lifting on his shirt collar. "Hello, schoolteacher," he said. His smile spread across his even teeth.

Lissa didn't think of Brandon as handsome, but he was ruggedly good-looking in his own way. Ever have enough money to buy himself a blue serge suit and get a regular haircut from a town barber, be surprised the difference it would make. Lissa knew that. She smiled back. Thunder rolled, jarring the ground. The sycamores tossed in the threatening wind.

"What brings you out on this road at four thirty?" Lissa asked, her fingers lifting from the steering wheel. Her smile widened.

"Why, I heard a calf bellowing and stepped across the pasture yonder to see if he was caught down here in the road fence." Brandon dipped his head, surveying them both as the thunder rolled again, and the wind twisted the car.

"Sure glad there's no calf hung up in a fence," Lissa said. She glanced out past Aunt Gustie. "You're right, Brandon, we may get a rain after all."

"Water in the bend's already rising. Must of had a downpour over west by Four Crossing."

"Well, Dodie Creek isn't White River or the Jordan. Think Mama's Ford'll crawl on across. Put her in low and crossed Dodie Creek many times in the rain." Her smile lingered on her lips.

The motor chugged, the wind dislodged a wisp of her hair. "Going my way, Brandon, hop in the back seat."

"Thanks, but got to head back to the place. Cut through here and round up the cows."

They lived only three miles apart, she and Brandon, though Dodie Creek lay between her mother Estra's farm and the Falls' weathered, native plank house and barn, perched on a rocky, mean hillside.

Lissa wanted to say a lot of things to Brandon Fall, but the approaching storm made her nervous. Ought to head on or she might not make it across the ford up ahead.

A howling wind shook the car and billowed Brandon's faded chambray shirt away from his chest, revealing muscular pectorals, in spite of his leanness.

"Better put her in gear and get across the ford. Wouldn't want you to meet Marla Edith Maggler on her way home from Dodder School. Way the water's rising, might crowd you into deep water." Brandon's dark eyes narrowed as his face tightened.

Lissa knew he was right. Twice she'd passed Marla Edith in the rocky creek bed. Even though Lissa had edged in first, Marla Edith never slowed her father's Buick touring car on the west bank. Plowed right in, water sloshing, horn blaring rudely. Made her stiffen and clutch the wheel. But Lissa had long ago decided not to be buffaloed by Marla Edith Maggler.

It was all over the school deal – Marla Edith accusing her of "stealing my school."

All Lissa had done was to grab an opportunity when Silas Whitsitt ambled up to her porch last May and offered her the contract at Blue Vale School for sixty dollars a month. The folks at home urged her to sign as they wrung their hands and praised the Lord. Now frail Estra Massey wouldn't be losing her farm after all, with Lissa bringing in regular money like that.

"But isn't Marla Edith going to teach at Blue Vale again next year?" Lissa had asked.

Board member Silas turned his broad face, hooked a thumb under a gallus, and said, "Well, now, there's been a change. Board thought Miss Marla Edith had too many relatives in Blue Vale School, her niece, Tippy Mae, and them Wincet cousins." He cleared his throat and looked down at the ground. "Twasn't the best thing for her or the scholars."

Lissa remembered Aunt Gustie's "a bird in the hand is worth two in the bush." She thought of her mother's pale face and thin body, rocking in the split-willow chair, owing seven hundred dollars on their valley farm. Lissa considered the offer an answer to prayer and signed. Marla Edith or no Marla Edith.

Questions still lingered. Just *why* didn't the board want Miss Maggler another year?

"Too many relatives in the school?" Aunt Gustie scoffed, a mist of spittle drifted. "Everyone knows them board members saw Marla Edith Maggler slip into the dance hall over in Ozark on a Saturday night last April. Black rayon dress, wobbling on her high heels, hanging on to Melvin Pempton's arm."

"But," Estra had said, "that didn't mean Marla Edith actually danced in the hall, did it?" It was not Estra's way to speak unkindly of anyone, even of old Sloan Maggler, who had foreclosed on Minnie and Siloam Hodge over past Four Crossing.

Lissa knew, though, that Marla Edith Maggler never admitted she'd been fired from Blue Vale school. "Opportunities were lacking there for someone like me with *forty* college hours." Marla had tossed her head, and her spit curl jarred loose. "Dodder School offered more opportunities for advancement, and besides, it's closer to Ozark, so I can get to the teachers' meetings without being late." At least, that's the way she explained it.

Lissa and everyone else knew that the board had threatened to close the tacky little Dodder school and unite it with the town school at Branson, and that Marla Edith had to make the best of a sorry situation even if it meant hunkering down and compromising herself.

Lissa wished her teaching job hadn't come about that way. In spite of her reserve, she had signed the little sweat-stained contract and thanked the Lord. Lissa put the Ford in gear and shoved in the clutch, remembering the rising water around the bend.

She glanced ahead where a dirt devil whipped and danced across a rocky swale. A heavy black car eased its long hood down the yellow rutted west bank of Dodie Creek.

"Well, so long, Brandon." She lifted her aching calf and let out the clutch.

Brandon raised his palm and ambled back to the sagging fence fringed with dying ragweed toward his motley cows. "You be careful now, Lissa." His voice drifted in the dust and wind.

Lissa brought the Ford to a halt on the right side of the road, staring at the black Essex rocking and groaning as it splashed into the creek.

"Why, that's Brother Stafford in that Essex, ain't it, Lissa?" Gustie leaned into the grasshopper-splattered windshield.

"Believe so. Way the water's rushing, I'd better wait until he eases through and climbs the grade." Lissa's fingers tightened on the wooden wheel. The Model A shook as the tiny motor clattered.

Then, to Lissa's dismay, Reverend Stafford's opulent black Essex coughed and died, wheels half-buried in the boiling water and sand. "Now what'll I do? Reverend Stafford stalled in the middle of the creek like that and Marla Edith Maggler soon plowing around the bend, blaring the horn of her father's new Buick." Lissa's heart palpitated. Aunt Gustie's brow creased, and her chin fell.

CHAPTER TWO

Reverend Wardley Stafford couldn't believe he was caught in such an embarrassing plight. A man in his station in life – sporting his second-to-best black serge, new black tie, and one of his starched white shirts fresh back from Tilda's Laundry. He raked his hand through his heavy salt-and-pepper hair.

Lord, now what? He couldn't be late for the roast pork supper at Amelia Longhorn's this evening. He'd considered staying on there until Sunday, when he would deliver his sermon to the good folks at White Oak, including the Masseys.

Maybe the folks over at Reeds Spring were right, pointing out that his mind wandered lately like a pasture calf separated from its mother. He knew he needed a wife, someone to help keep his mind on the practical things of life. But his dear Myrna'd been lying in Rose Cemetery now for three years, and he was still single.

He stared at the Model A shuddering across Dodie Creek on the left bank, where a young woman driver perched alongside some wizened old Ozark woman.

* * *

Lissa opened the Ford's thin door, and her small foot, graced in a brown pump, slid out. She cupped a hand at her mouth and called, "Reverend Stafford, what can we do?" A burst of wind whipped the young woman's skirt around her calves. The water roared.

Lissa stared at the eddies rising around the Essex's wheels, her brow wrinkling. Her heart thumped as the polished door opened and the powerful man stepped out, black pants rolled above his calves, his broad bare feet sousing down into the water.

Lissa knew Reverend Stafford, who had been in top leadership position in the church district for the past ten years, would be humiliated by this predicament.

"Better wait there, Reverend." Lissa's throat tightened, her mind whirled. What can I do?

"Lissa, ain't you got a chain in the tool box on the fender out here?" Aunt Gustie coughed and steadied her chin.

"Why, you're the Massey girl, aren't you?" Stafford's booming preacher's voice echoed above the water's roar. Wardley gripped the shiny Essex fender sporting the bulging nickel headlights to steady himself. He picked his way toward the front of his car.

"Good thing you pulled over and stopped there, young lady. My, my, my, who'd have ever...." His worried voice was overshadowed by a clap of thunder.

"Reverend Stafford, I've got a chain in my tool box. Just stay right there. Water might be too deep. Think I can step out partway, throw you the chain, and back the Ford up and pull you on through."

At least it was worth a try. What if a heavy rain let loose and the churchman's Essex toppled and floated on down the raging torrent?

Lissa turned toward her open car door, unhooked her garters, stripped down her seamed hose, letting them drop onto her dusty shoes by a Russian thistle. Preacher or no preacher looking on. She fished through the dusty toolbox, fingers tightening around the chain. Hook end of the heavy chain in hand, she stepped gingerly over the gravel to the edge of the roaring water.

"You ain't going out in them swells and riffles, are you, girl?" Aunt Gustie bobbed and rocked, eyes wide, hand clutching at her weathered neck.

Lissa jumped at another clap of thunder, but she managed to hold on to the heavy chain. Her blue and pink-striped rayon dress whipped at the back of her thighs and billowed at her bosom as the rain started to pelt her.

"I'm going to wade in a ways. I'll watch my step. Dodie Creek and I are old friends, Reverend Stafford. Don't you fear. When I'm about halfway over, believe if you reach out in front of your Essex, you can grab the chain and hook it up."

Lissa's voice trembled as she stepped deeper into the swift-flowing water. What if I fall? Slip on a rock? What if the water washes my feet out from under me?

She clamped her teeth as her feet plunged into the roiling water. Couldn't give up without a try. Hadn't she scraped and saved and pushed herself, getting those twenty college hours at the Normal School? Let alone signing that Blue Vale school contract, Marla Edith or no Marla Edith.

Her left foot slid off a slime-covered rock. Lissa staggered. The weight of the chain almost pulled her into the rushing swirls, but she regained her footing, heart in her throat. The wind dislodged more wisps of her blond hair, which flapped in her eyes.

"Catch the hook, Reverend Stafford." Lissa leaned forward and heaved the clanking chain. The smell of fish and rotting leaves rose to her nostrils, mingling with the dusty, fresh drifts of the rain, plastering her dress to her back. She flinched as lightning cracked. She glanced at Reverend Stafford hanging on to the front of his car. Why hadn't he taken off his coat? She noticed that his square shoulders swung youthfully for a man his age. His granite jaw lifted as he called, "Bless the Lord, Miss Massey. I've caught it!"

Then his right foot slipped off a slimy rock beneath the current. He staggered, tilted, and stumbled before he grabbed a shiny headlight and caught himself.

"Whoooooh, Miss Massey, fella's got to watch it. Bend over and hook her up somewhere under here." His voice lowered in the wind as the rumble of an engine drifted toward them and Marla Edith Maggler rounded the bend, steering her father's glistening Buick to a halt on the west bank.

"Pont, pont, pont," blared her horn. Marla Edith leaned her black-haired head with its plastered spit curl out the open window. "Well, I declare." She slid out of the front seat of the purring Buick, evidently unconcerned about the blowing rain drenching her rayon sleeveless dress when faced with such a challenge.

"That you, Lissa Massey? Feature that." Marla Edith stared at her and shouted. "You're going to fall! Foolish, foolish...." The thunder clapped. The back of Elder Stafford's Essex shifted to the right as the current increased.

"Reverend Stafford, can you hear me? Wait in your car until the water goes down. Lissa's not going to be able to help you. Foolishness. Foolishness. If only I could get a rope. That tinny Ford of hers wouldn't pull open the sow pen gate." Marla Edith had both hands on her hips, seemingly not minding at all, casting a slur to the wind, letting it drift across, preacher or no preacher. Marla Edith slid back into her father's plush-seated Buick. By that time, Lissa had crawled into her mother's Ford, engine still puttering. She had forgotten to step into her slippers, and the clutch pedal hurt her foot.

"Why, Lissa Massey, you don't know how to...." Aunt Gustie's voice drifted above the roar of the waters.

Lissa yelled out the open window, "Ready, Brother Stafford? Going to put it in reverse and try to pull you right on through." Her voice quivered. Her knees knocked. A cold shiver swept over her.

Her fingers tightened around the marbled-glass bulb of the gearshift. Where was reverse? Gears ground as she searched. If only her legs would stop trembling. Lissa released the clutch, but too abruptly. The Ford coughed and died.

"Pont, pont!" sounded Marla's horn from the farther side, conveying the clear message that slow-witted Lissa Massey didn't even know how to find reverse, let alone let out the clutch.

Lissa, her face set like Aunt Gustie's when she worried about whether or not she had forgotten to put baking soda in her biscuits, bore down with her bare heel on the little round metal starter. She winced as pain shot up her calf, gripped the wooden wheel, and bared down again.

"Gurrr-rrr-rrrrr...." The car backfired and started. Again, the grinding, as she searched for reverse. "Dear Lord, let it work this time."

Lissa let out the clutch, easier the second time, as her clutch leg had stopped most of its trembling and jumping around.

The chain tightened. She hoped it wouldn't break and clang back like the time Lit Watson tried to move his chicken house and the chain spiraled back and smashed his windshield to smithereens.

Tires dug down into the wet sand. They spun. The front end of the Model A reared.

The Essex lurched. Reverend Stafford, subdued as a catbird with salt on its tail, guided his rocking car as if it still had full power. He gripped the wheel, leaning forward as the long car sagged momentarily, then began to ease across flooding Dodie Creek.

The little Ford bucked. The wheels threw sand. Lissa held on to the trembling and lurching Model A. "Lord, Lord, let me get him up the grade before a log sails downstream and sends him to perdition."

Suddenly it was over. The Essex, up out of the water, leaned at the side of the road. Lissa's little Ford finished its bucking, though the steam boiling out the radiator cap up front would have made Old Faithful ashamed.

Elder Stafford eased his brawny, bare feet out from the purple floor carpet to the runningboard. He lifted his powerful body, rubbed his jaw to check the five o'clock shadow. "Well, Miss Massey, you are a wonder. I'll unhook your chain. You'd better turn your mother's Ford around and drive on up after me to Amelia Longhorn's place till the water subsides." He raked a hand through his heavy hair.

Lissa saw that the episode had wilted him considerably. Still, his dark eyes beneath heavy brows gleamed like black onyx. Certitude seemed still on the shelf of his psyche, though slightly off center.

Reverend Stafford cleared his throat. The chain banged and rattled. His hand clasped the belt of his lean waist. He hadn't allowed himself a bulging spread or potbelly, like some men his age sported.

"Let me put the chain back into your toolbox, Miss Massey. My, how shall I ever repay you?" He looked down at the veins and cords in his feet, then tilted his chin again.

"And Miss Massey, I shall have to ask your pardon about my bare feet." His husky voice drifted in the wind.

"Well, it worked, didn't it? I'm glad I could help you, Reverend Stafford." Lissa chuckled nervously. "I'll be looking forward to hearing you preach, come Sunday. Aunt Gustie and I'll just wait here. The rain's blown over. We sure needed it."

Reverend Stafford's pants bagged and his wet coat fluttered as he tried to ease himself back into his sagging Essex with dignity. He bore down on the starter. The prolonged low growl told them he'd have to wait until the spark plugs dried off.

"Pont pont!" Marla Edith eased her long-hooded Buick on in. "Ought to have a Buick like this," she called out the open window. She leaned into the windshield as the car rocked in low gear. With bigger wheels, and higher up off the ground, the Buick lunged like a longhorn steer crossing White River.

Lissa leaped out of her Ford to retrieve her stockings and shoes. She turned and saw Brandon Fall loping down the road toward them. He hadn't even gotten around to finishing buttoning his shirt.

"Heard horns honking and thought you'd been caught in Dodie Creek, Lissa. Thank God you're all right." Brandon's hair stood up in the wind like John Brown's of Bleeding Kansas.

Lissa snatched her stockings and shoes, stepping back as Marla Edith's Buick groaned and lurched straight at her. She turned, stockings whipping in the breeze, to call out: "Brandon, you can get into my car. I'll drive you on back to your place. That way, the water'll be safe when I come back."

By now Marla Edith had stopped the Buick, a little orange perch still flopping on the running board, broad smile on her olive-skinned face, spit curl springing.

"Why, Brandon, jump in my Buick. I'm headed your way. Drop you off. You ever ridden in a Buick?"

Lissa noticed Marla Edith glare at her before she turned her slick smile on Brandon.

"Well, yes, Marla, er, ah … thank you." Brandon shrugged his shoulders, and when Marla Edith leaned over in her damp black sleeveless and opened the passenger side door, he sauntered over and slid in. He called across to Lissa, "This way, Lissa, I won't make you late. Know your brother Slade and your mother'll be waiting for you. Tell them I said hello. Brandon waved to Lissa from the Buick window. Then he lifted a brown farmer's hand to Wardley Stafford as Marla Edith gunned the Buick, sand spitting. Brandon's voice drifted back, "Surely looking forward to your next sermon, Brother Stafford."

By the time Wardley Stafford tried his Essex the third time, it backfired, and the motor took hold on two cylinders, then three, then all six.

"Bless the Lord, Miss Massey. Bless the Lord. Tell you what I plan to do. Take you and your dear mother, Estra, and your brother, Slade – Aunt Gustie, too – over to Ophelia's Restaurant on Main there in Springfield to repay you." He beamed above a solid, cleft chin.

Lissa Massey gripped the Ford's wheel, mouth a straight line. The shuddering little car groaned and splashed its way on across Dodie Creek. Just why did she suddenly feel so hollow inside?

CHAPTER THREE

Lissa slammed the Model A door, grabbed her floppy book satchel. Left shoulder sagging, she clutched a stack of papers at her bosom. She traipsed up the flagstone walk, fringed with dry crabgrass and an old, drought-resistant rosebush sporting one frazzled yellow rose. Lissa hated being late. Meant her brother, Slade, had to fill in the cracks milking Molly and Clementine.

Her head ached and her fingers throbbed from clenching the Ford's steering wheel so tightly while rescuing Reverend Stafford and his Essex. Echoes from Marla Edith's "pont ponting" horn and flashes of Marla Edith whisking Brandon off in her father's opulent Buick caused a pain to shoot through her head. She would try to forget Marla Edith's slurs about her mother's Ford.

Why did Elder Stafford's face loom before her, chiseled, mature, the handsome salt-and-pepper hair? No hint of baldness like so many men his age. Was that bay rum lotion that seemed to still linger?

Well, the young men she knew didn't have extra money for lotions. When she had held the tattered songbook with Brandon Fall in services two weeks back, all she smelled was the strong aroma of Lifebuoy Soap.

Lissa and Aunt Gustie dragged into the kitchen. Lissa tromped up the narrow stairs to her room while Aunt Gustie limped to the hook behind the door and grabbed an apron.

Upstairs, Lissa thought about how ridiculous it was the way the women of the Sewing Circle gossiped about Wardley Stafford.

Widows dipping their heads, trying not to skip a stitch at the mention of a lonely churchman who deserved a full home, wife included. She smiled at the thought of plain-faced Amelia Longhorn fussing over her roast pork dinner. Amelia – one of four in the church who'd never married.

Then, too, there was the time Sam Mabley set foot under Amelia's table. After supper, Amelia dragged out a bowl of cracked black walnuts and Sam had to sit there and pick kernels in front of the fireplace while he tried to think of something to say to beaming Amelia. How was Elder Stafford faring this evening?

Who am I to call Amelia plain? Lissa caught a glimpse of her tanned face in the hall mirror. Pinned-up hair, wisps tangled by the wind. More toward the plain side myself. Cheekbones lack prominence and my chin is a bit too long, isn't it?

Of course, Lissa had never tried lipstick or rouge to bring out her cheekbones. Her mother always said, "Lissa, you have the Massey features, like your father, fine features."

She reckoned troubling herself over such trivialities was wasted time.

Lissa hung her damp dress and stockings to dry on a wooden hanger behind the door and tightened the belt buckle of her blue calico frock. She picked her way down the darkening, narrow stairway. Her white-haired mother, Estra, standing in front of the Home Comfort range, turned around from stirring her green beans. "Why, Lissa. I worried about you. Little rain like that didn't make Dodie Creek come up much, did it?"

Lissa's soft eyes fell on her mother's lined face, white hair drawn back in a bun. Lissa noticed the tremor in her mother's hand as she held the wooden spoon.

How frail she's getting since Papa died last April. Bereavement still squeezed Lissa's heart. It'd been only lately that she could go into her parents' bedroom where her father, Jesse Massey, a prominent farmer in the valley, suffered and died from throat cancer.

A sense of thankfulness spread over Lissa for such a good and loving mother and father. There wasn't time for a full acknowledgment of the thought, but it was there in her heart.

"Downpour over west, Mother. You wouldn't believe how fast

Dodie Creek came up."

"You didn't try to cross it when it was dangerous, did you, Lissa? Lots of folks' cars stall when they plunge on in without thinking." Estra's eyebrows lifted.

Aunt Gustie, clutching a bowl of green beans, cleared her throat. "You don't know your daughter, Estra."

Before Lissa could reply, the door to the back porch flew open as her eleven-year-old brother, Slade, strode across the blue and yellow linoleum, brown eyes wide, red lips breaking into a smile.

"Thought you'd never get home, Lissa. Went ahead and milked Molly and Clementine for you. I already ran the milk through the cream separator."

Lissa stepped over to the overall-clad boy, brushed back his cowlick with her fingers.

"Thank you, Slade. Knew I could depend on you." She tried not to sag too much from the day's challenges or the thought of those arithmetic papers she still had to grade by lamplight after the dishes were washed.

Their mouths watered as they glanced at the mashed potatoes and green beans. Estra placed the platter with the sliced meatloaf near Slade's plate. Aunt Gustie hobbled around the table, favoring the foot that still bothered her from the needle she'd stepped on back in 1919.

Lissa felt sorry for Aunt Gustie, living alone across the footbridge on the bank of Dodie Creek in her three-room cottage, trumpet vine smothering it. Though they all, at times, rankled at Aunt Gustie's scathing tongue.

"We've got to help Aunt Gustie through her years," her father, Jesse, had said. "She gives us side-splitting laughs. Besides, the Lord loves Aunt Gustie."

Lissa glanced at Slade, feeling the warmth of his goodness – how he treasured the Bible given to him when he advanced to the third-grade class at White Oak Sunday School.

Estra called on Lissa to say grace as the four bowed their heads reverently in the light of the coal oil lamp, which cast a soft glow from the center of the table.

Their ears tuned to the clank of fork on plate and spoon. Aunt

Gustie at the west end, elbows weighing down the table, calico dust cap twisted on her head, insisted on forking her vittles with a black wooden-handled fork. Her chin dropped as she opened her thin lips to poke in a morsel of pork she'd found in her green beans.

"That Elder Stafford otta knew better'n to plunge into that creek. Amelia Longhorn's victuals – that's what drew him." She cackled and grinned over the spaces where her front teeth were missing.

"That's right, Aunt Gustie, and Reverend Stafford's scheduled to preach this Sunday." Lissa forked a portion of the spicy meatloaf. "Wouldn't it be interesting if he asked Brandon to preach, instead?"

Slade laid down his fork. "That explains the ruckus. Clementine wouldn't come in for milking, so I had to hurry way out west toward that persimmon patch to get her. Quite a fracas going on way over there on the banks of Dodie Creek where Route Seven crosses the ford. Was that our Model A, Lissa?" Slade's blue eyes searched Lissa's face.

Lissa raked a wisp of hair, sipped from her pressed-glass water tumbler, and said, "It was Aunt Gustie and me, Slade. Actually, I was quite worried. That downpour over by Four Crossing caused a sudden rise over the Dodie Creek ford."

"You can say that again. Worry the life out of an old soul like me." Aunt Gustie cackled, laying down her half-slice of bread, spread with butter and molasses.

"Well, how fortunate our church is to have an Elder like Reverend Stafford with us so often." Estra's soft brown eyes lifted in the lamplight. "I always take a marking pencil and mark my Bible when he preaches."

"Well, he preaches too long some Sundays," Slade said, stabbing at a pickled red beet. "But I wish I was old enough to vote. I'd vote for Brandon Fall to be our minister. I like his sermons better."

"Elder Stafford has such a cultivated voice, suited for reading the Scriptures," his mother added. "One of the finest graduates of his seminary class down in Memphis in his day. Too bad about losing his beloved Myrna."

Her voice faltered, as they all had memory of recent death. Estra glanced at the door of the room where her own fifty-three-year-old Jessee died last year. Lissa knew her mother was trying not to let the weight of the Depression and hard times drag her down.

"Was that Miss Maggler's Buick roaring down Number Seven with Brandon Fall sitting in it?" Slade asked.

"Well, yes, Slade. Yes, it was. We had quite a meeting there on the banks of Dodie Creek," Lissa picked through her green beans. Now that Slade had ripped things open, she'd have to wade on in and answer their questions.

"Har, har, har." Aunt Gustie wiped her mouth with the back of a liver-spotted hand. "Miss Marla?" She let the word slide out like the hiss of a puff adder.

Estra faced Gustie. "We need to say nice things about–"

"Miss Marla Edith Maggler and her old Pap's Buick? Yep. I can understand why Marla Maggler'd load up Brandon Fall. Heee hee, hee. Why, old as I am, I'd be tempted to tote Brandon Fall around myself. Course I ain't got no car."

"A car is a big expense, Aunt Gustie," Slade said, "You'd–"

"Do you think he'd take a ride in my wheelbarrow?" Gustie slapped her lean thigh and cackled.

Now, everyone laid down fork, knife, or spoon and stared at Lissa.

"Was the Reverend actually stuck in the ford?" Estra asked, her brow creased.

"Sorry to say, yes, Mother, his Essex drowned out. Though I understand, Reverend Stafford not being very familiar with Dodie Creek and that crossing." Something in her wanted to protect the distinguished man.

Before supper ended, Lissa had to go over all the details. She started chuckling as she remembered how she unhooked her garters and stripped off her stockings, Reverend Stafford or no Reverend Stafford.

After all, it was the sensible thing to do, everyone delayed by the mishap, Brandon sliding into Marla Edith's car that way, wasn't it? Saved her from turning around and making herself even later.

She'd offered him a ride back to Amelia's, but instead, he did climb into that Buick with Marla Edith, didn't he? Lissa decided not to dwell on it as she rose and began to clear the table.

CHAPTER FOUR

After supper that evening, Aunt Gustie picked her way through moonlight and shadows as she limped across the footbridge over Dodie Creek to her cottage. She fingered the twenty-five cent piece in her apron pocket that Estra had given her for two quarts of her pickled red beets, as Estra's beets withered and dried up in her garden. Gustie's tongue slid across the gap left by her two missing front teeth as she thought of the twenty dollars she'd saved for the blessed day when she could afford her store teeth. Tuck the quarter away in that bent little Prince Albert tobacco box under her bed.

* * *

Lissa washed the dishes in the blue granite dishpan and Slade dried them, while Estra stacked the bowls and plates in the oak curved glass cupboard. A nighthawk called, and cattle lowed in the distance. The breeze, heavy with the smell of dried-up corn, floated through the dining room door.

After Lissa had graded the arithmetic papers at the round kitchen table in the lamplight, she stacked them neatly and stuffed them in her satchel by the stand table. She rose, stretched her arms while glancing out the dining room window to the moonlit yard and pasture. Warm enough yet to sit a while in the moonlight on the porch swing.

On the porch, Lissa's eyes swept over the barnyard and the nearly dried-up pond, the brown pasture grass, a silvery patina in the moonlight. Now and then a late frog in the muddy pond shallows croaked for rain. Cicadas' piercing chirps answered the frogs. A sudden wind rattled the drying leaves in the white oak in the yard by the flagstone walk.

Lissa settled herself on the porch swing, one foot pushing to a slow glide. Weariness from the day eased out of her body as she sat, embraced by the balmy wind and the night sounds.

She turned her head toward the path leading from the backyard when she heard the rustle of leaves and gravel.

"Evening, Lissa. Don't want to startle you." Brandon Fall slipped around the house, scraping past the overhanging bowers of the trumpet vine. He paused to break off a cluster of three orange blossoms, luminescent in the moonlight.

"Why, Brandon. I'm glad you walked over." Her hand rose to smooth her hair.

Lissa knew Brandon often went for early night walks, loving nature as he did. Also, he needed time to put it all together, the heaviness of his responsibilities of trying to make a living on forty acres and care for his father, Owney, paralyzed on his left side, now, for two years. Guided his mother, Serena, too, through it. Poor woman, chest caved in, back bent from picking cotton when she was a girl in Arkansas.

"Why, Brandon. Come on up and have a seat." She patted the space on the porch swing beside her as his heavy work brogues hit the unpainted steps. Her eyes lingered on his rugged, lean face, hair still damp from his evening bath. Sporting clean striped overalls with only one patch on the left knee. Sweetness of sun-dried laundry lingered on his blue chambray shirt. Her heart warmed and her tiredness drifted away.

The swing creaked as Brandon lowered himself and crossed one lanky leg over another, revealing the patch.

The moment hung. Was it his shyness? Or was it Lissa's? Somewhere over by Dodie Creek, a whippoorwill called to its mate.

"Something I wanted to tell you, Lissa. This evening Deacon Whitsitt stopped in, said Reverend Stafford called him from Amelia's place and asked him to see if I could preach this Sunday."

He shifted his leg.

"Oh," Lissa said, eyes widening, "I thought Brother Stafford was scheduled to preach Sunday."

"Well, whatever the mixup, they must have straightened it out. Brother Whitsitt insisted on me. Said Reverend Stafford wanted to hear me give a sermon." Brandon lowered his head and cleared his throat.

"That's good news, Brandon." Lissa looked down at his work-scarred hands and realized she sat beside a young man more suited for the scholars' rooms in libraries and archives, studying theology, Greek, and Hebrew. She realized she and Brandon were far removed from anything resembling that these days.

"Have you selected your text?" Lissa wanted to encourage him, remembering how his mellow voice carried in their church, and how the folks welcomed his words.

"Thinking of something from Philippians. Brother Supple told the deacons he's thinking of retiring since he turned seventy. I guess they want to see if the Lord is leading me, and if they want to ordain me in the future." Brandon cleared his throat, clasping the porch swing chain in one hand, dark eyes focused on Lissa. Lissa noticed his eyes search her face while one finger stroked the trumpet vine blossom in his overall bib pocket.

Brandon glanced down at her small hands, folded in her lap. What *did* he think of her? At least Brandon knew she was hard-working and determined, didn't he?

The silence hung. The cicadas chirped. Lissa, aware of his bashful affection for her, glanced at his eyes, noticing how they looked cobalt in the evening light.

"God will help you find a way. The drought won't last forever. Some seminaries offer scholarships, Brandon. I know you would qualify," she smiled.

"I have hope. But sometimes, needy as my family is on our forty, I think of signing up for the Civilian Conservation Corps along with Smitty Thomas and Loren Wagner. At least they send home twenty dollars a month."

Lissa turned to face him. "Brandon, White Oak Church – that's a real opportunity for you."

"It's a possibility. Course, if they ordain me and want me to preach steadily, I'd still have to get up to Springfield to the Bible College. But close as it is, I could do both."

A vision of Marla Edith Maggler loading Brandon in her Buick flashed through Lissa's mind. She wanted to talk to him about the Magglers and how Marla Edith goaded her about "stealing my school." Lissa tried to forgive Marla Edith and go on, especially since Tiphanie Mae, Marla Edith's niece, whom everybody called Tippy Mae, was one of her own eighth-graders.

"You're fortunate to have a good job, Lissa, and Ruth Harrison told me down at Watson's store that you're the best teacher Eva Ruth and Celeste ever had."

"Well, I'm glad to hear that, Brandon. I'm just a beginner, you know." Her voice dropped. "But you know, Marla Edith is still angry with me, and having Tippy Mae in my school complicates matters. I wish her parents would be more concerned about her. The way they send that girl to school in Marla Edith's old cast-offs." Lissa wanted to say more about Marla's brother, Bart, and his slovenly wife, Mertice, and how some folks believed that Tippy Mae was simply old Bart Maggler's scullery maid.

"Bart Maggler neglects his family, I'm sorry to say, Lissa." Brandon straightened his back against the slats.

"It makes it worse, my brother, Slade, a student in Marla Edith's school."

"Have to walk a tight rope, don't you, Lissa? Well, after what you did today, pulling Reverend Stafford on through flooding Dodie Creek, I'd say you know how to walk tight ropes." He smiled, showing his white, even teeth. He stretched an arm on the back of the swing behind her, then removed it, clearing his throat.

The whippoorwills called again, and a cooler wind carrying the musty smell of cattails from the nearly dry pond swept over the porch. She sensed that Brandon wanted to say more, or even reach down with his callused hand and envelope her own hands in his. Instead, he gently lifted her fingers and dropped the sprig of trumpet vine with the three orange blossoms into her pale, upturned palm.

Brandon rose to go. "Good night, Lissa." His voice caught as he inhaled the night air. Was it a sigh?

"Why, good night, Brandon. Sure you have to leave so early?" Her hand automatically reached upwards. Why is his face suddenly so serious? But before an answer slid to her mind, she realized he was bending over her. She felt the heat of his face and the trace of his warm lips on her cheek. Then he was at the bottom of the porch steps.

Caught by surprise, Lissa called out, "I'll pray for you, Brandon. I'll see you at church on Sunday." She stood, one arm braced against the lathe-turned porch post, wondering why she was trembling.

With three long strides, Brandon disappeared around the corner past the trumpet vine, heading for the footbridge over Dodie Creek.

CHAPTER FIVE

The smell of orchid toilet water wafted through Marla Edith Maggler's upstairs bedroom. Irritation nipped as she slipped her deep red dress with the shawl sleeves over her head. Why had she slept so late, with Brandon preaching today at White Oak? Ida Lou Swank, who played that ancient little pump organ, bumped into her at the grocery store and announced in her singsong voice, "You oughta come and hear our Brandon, Miss Maggler."

Well, Marla Edith planned to make it. No, Pa Maggler didn't need the Buick today, did he? Anyway, she decided to grab it first as he had loped out with his rifle for an early squirrel hunt. Marla was glad she had Cecilia redo her hair and get rid of the spit curl.

Marla Edith eyed her shiny black hair in her hand mirror. Yes, I like the bangs better than the spit curl. And the way it's taken a curl, won't need a snood in the back.

She checked her hose seams in the mirror, brushing her fingers over her fleshy calves, then eased her feet into her high-heeled pumps. Nothing like high-heeled pumps to make a woman feel like a lady, she had decided a long time ago.

Her purse banged a thigh and her keys jangled as she hurried down the stairs, taking care not to turn her ankle. If Brandon doesn't preach at White Oak today, then at least I'll get to hear that distinguished-looking Wardley Stafford with the Clark Gable face. She gave her hair a reassuring pat.

Encouraged by her thoughts, she gripped the Buick's ivory wheel

A BRANSON LOVE

and turned it down the curving road toward White Oak Church.

Marla Edith realized she was a little late, but the singing hadn't begun yet. She braked and turned the Buick into a space between Reverend Stafford's Essex and Deacon Whitsitt's dusty Chevrolet by the rough-barked persimmon trees. To the far right of the churchyard, she spied Brandon Fall's decrepit Model T tilting like a weathered privy. Pity, the way he has to work to start it. Jack one wheel off the ground, race around, and crank the engine. Drive off the jack. Stop, hurry back, and retrieve the jack. Then, if the car was still running, hop back in. Marla hated the lean cold hands of poverty, though she didn't blame Brandon.

Marla Edith stepped with her heavy-hipped sway down the sandy path toward the church. She spied a group of five young men catching up on the latest baseball scores before they entered the sanctuary. She sniffed as drifts of musty hymnals and old wood varnish hit her nose. Rearing her head, she clutched her black purse under her left arm, right arm swinging freely in order to show the young blades how a lady walks in high heels.

Marla Edith composed her painted lips and batted her eyelids, aware of the folks watching her slide onto a bench. She squeezed in behind forty-year-old Clip Hooter, the widower she'd dated a time or two, sitting with his three-year-old son, Ned. She decided if Clip turned to glance at her, she would smile at him.

* * *

Lissa and Estra sat on the other side of the church. Pity for Marla Edith rose in Lissa's breast. Lonely, she's lonely and desperate. That's why she's here. Who's she got her eye on today? Brandon, or Reverend Stafford?

Ida Lou Swank, perched on the little plush-covered stool, leaned towards her hymnal and began to play *What a Friend We Have in Jesus*. Lissa lifted her voice to join the hundred or more hearty singers.

By the time Reverend Stafford read from Psalms and their own kindly Brother Supple introduced the preacher of the day, Brandon Fall, Lissa's mind eased. She let go of her tenseness about Marla

Edith. She prayed for her when they recited the Lord's Prayer. "Forgive us our trespasses as we forgive those who trespass against us."

Lissa noticed Estra lean forward for Brandon's sermon. Slade, too, over on the left. Her heart warmed at how Slade loved the things of the church and carried his Bible faithfully.

Lissa knew Brandon's worn brown suit was the only one he had. The clean white shirt and the plain brown tie, however, helped. His deep-timbred voice carried throughout the church as he read from Philippians: "Rejoice in the Lord alway: and again I say, Rejoice. Let your moderation be known unto all men. The Lord is at hand."

Brandon's brown eyes focused on his Bible and notes, then he lifted his head to survey the congregation as he unfolded the thoughts God had given him on the passage.

A good sermon, thought Lissa. Three points. Way a sermon ought to be. Gives a body something to take home. Points helpful for everyone present, including herself. Lately she hadn't remembered to rejoice always as St. Paul commanded. That meant even when the sun dried and curled the corn leaves, and when others hurled insults and accused you, falsely, of lying.

When the service was over, Reverend Wardley Stafford boomed the benediction in his resonate voice, chin thrust outward, eyes closed. "The Lord bless thee and...."

"My, doesn't Reverend Stafford have a marvelous voice?" Edith Tilldon whispered to Lissa.

"And," said Margarite Garrelson, "that boyfriend of yours, Lissa, Brandon Fall, surely gave us a fine sermon, didn't he? Rejoice. Be moderate, and remember – Jesus is nearby."

"He did, Margarite, yes, it was well-outlined, and Brandon has good...."

"Please find Brandon, Lissa," Estra said. "I'm inviting Reverend Stafford for fried chicken dinner, and I want Brandon to come too."

Several minutes passed before Lissa's turn at the vestibule where Wardley Stafford and Brandon stood side by side shaking hands with folks of the congregation.

Lissa, seeing her mother approaching the distinguished elder, made a quick trip to the primary Sunday school room to see if the picture cards for next week's lesson had arrived in the mail.

When she returned, Estra stood visiting with Reverend Stafford. He bowed, nodded his head, and beamed, "Well, well, yes, Sister Estra. Chicken dinner at your home, how could I turn that down?"

"I'll bet Wardley Stafford is hoping someone will invite him before Amelia Longhorn wades through the crowd and snags him," Sam Mabley whispered to a neighbor. "I never want to pick walnut kernels at her house again long as I live."

"Did you ask Brandon?" Estra clasped Lissa's arm with her white-gloved hand.

"Mother, he must have slipped out before you got to the vestibule." Then she spotted the worn brown suit, wide pant legs flapping in the wind, his dark brown hair curling on his neck. "Why, there he is out by Marla Edith's Buick. Look at that, she's got the hood up and Brandon's leaning over the motor. Can't she get a new car like that started?" Lissa's hand shifted to her mouth.

The young preacher-to-be slammed the hood shut, loped around the back to the driver's side, and slid under the wheel. The starter ground, the motor purred. Lissa noticed that Marla Edith had already thrust herself on the passenger side, her shiny hair tossing in the open window as the wine-colored car headed down the stretch of gravel toward Ozark, or maybe even to Springfield.

I can't believe it. Brandon's hands clasping that ivory wheel?

CHAPTER SIX

Lissa parked her mother's Model A in the faded red garage by the locust trees. Her coattail lifted in the wind as her heels pounded the flagstones leading to the gabled house. She lifted her eyes and noticed the paint peeling on the eaves. Painting would have to wait for better times. Marla Edith? Brandon? Where? I'll bet over to that Ophelia's Restaurant. Her brow furrowed.

In the sunlit kitchen, Lissa placed her Bible and Sunday School quarterly on the edge of the yellow oak buffet, pulled a cabinet drawer open, and yanked out her cobbler's apron with the strawberry applique. She whipped it open.

"Lissa, Brandon'll be back in time for evening services at Reeds Spring. We'll enjoy visiting with Reverend Stafford along with Slade and Aunt Gustie. I'll get the range stoked up. You best get the chicken on."

Why did Mother have to mention Brandon? Lissa remembered she did have company and made an attempt to smile and be gracious, even though she still felt awkward over her encounter on Dodie Creek with Reverend Stafford a week ago.

While Slade entertained Reverend Stafford with his moth and butterfly collection, the sounds of pan lids, pokers on stove grates, and the clang of the pitcher pump echoed in the kitchen.

Lissa dipped a fresh chicken leg into buttermilk, rolled it into the peppered and salted flour and edged the piece into the iron skillet as the grease sizzled.

Lissa's lips sagged at the corners. Have to try and loosen up a bit with Reverend Stafford here.

* * *

Heavenly aroma rose from the fried chicken platter. Mashed potatoes laced with melting butter filled the Dresden bowl with the burgundy rose splashed along the side. Bright green sweet pickles contrasted with the shiny pickled red beets.

Aunt Gustie hunched low in her chair at the south end of the ecru linen-covered table, her plate hiding the patch. Slade, across from Reverend Stafford, Estra at the head, and Lissa, seated by Slade, faced the smiling minister.

Following the Reverend's prayer of thanks, which Lissa thought was too long, they lifted their heads and unfolded their napkins.

Lissa forgot her disappointment when the conversation turned to her daring rescue of Reverend Wardley. She chuckled when she thought of her bare feet and trailing stockings.

"Our Lissa is a brave, hardworking girl, Reverend Stafford." Estra reached for the peas and onions.

"Well, Marla Edith Maggler's pont, ponting horn made Miss Lissa and me step lively in the water." Reverend Stafford wiped his handsome mouth with an ecru napkin, lips curved in a smile.

Lissa put down her fork. She couldn't help looking at him – broad-shouldered, sturdy. A healthy man, whose years, in spite of his recent widowhood, hadn't taken their toll.

"Well, I'll tell you something," Aunt Gustie said. "You ain't gonna get no real help from Marla Edith Maggler until the water goes down." She pointed with the black-handled fork for emphasis. "Now you take our Lissa, the Dodie Creek ford ain't the only thing she's plunged into."

It seemed as if Aunt Gustie was leading the conversation in a threatening direction, but Estra interrupted.

"Well, all are safe. That's the important thing. Lissa, Miss Maggler, and Reverend Stafford. As Brandon preached this morning, 'the Lord is at hand.'" She lifted her eyes to catch a glimpse of the Reverend Stafford's good-looking face, lips curving like the road into Branson.

After the scrumptious Sunday dinner, Reverend Stafford patted his lips with his napkin and pushed back from the table.

"My, my, ladies, Estra, Lissa, you too, Aunt Gustie. My, my. Even in hard times, you folks know how to feed a preacher."

Estra stood, dismissing the table. "So glad you enjoyed the meal, Reverend Stafford. We'd hoped that Brandon would join us too, however...." Estra's face betrayed that she wished she hadn't added the last sentence.

Aunt Gustie poked at a back tooth with a fingernail, then focused her grey eyes on Wardley Stafford's lean waist.

"Well, now, Reverend." She stared. "You ain't got no potbelly like a lot of men your age. Compliment to you. Why yes, you're a young looker, for sure, for your age." She snickered and looked up at Lissa to see if she'd gotten a rise out of her.

"Why, Gustie Simpson, thank you for the compliment." Wardley Stafford looked over at a blushing Lissa. "Your Aunt Gustie's got a real sense of humor, hasn't she, Lissa?"

After the dishes were washed and put away, the blue enamel dishpan hung under the dry sink, and the sun came out, warming the air, Wardley Stafford said, "Believe I'll stretch my legs awhile, Slade, Lissa." He opened the screen door and strode out on the wide porch where the silver lace vine wound up the trellis.

Estra nodded to Lissa, which meant, "Go on out on the porch, we can't let the Reverend stand out there by himself."

So Lissa, whose tongue suddenly stuck to the roof of her mouth, stepped out onto the wide porch planks with him, hands clasped behind her back. A balmy wind billowed her blue skirt. She caught the spicy drift of the purple chrysanthemums by the old well.

"My, my, splendid afternoon." He surveyed a group of swallows sweeping toward the barn. "Why, Miss Lissa, believe it's a perfect day for an afternoon walk." Wardley stretched his shoulders.

"It's a fine day, Reverend Stafford." Now what shall I do? Lissa stared at a red squirrel which seemed to be mocking her, flashing its tail, chattering straight at her.

"Brother Stafford, wouldn't you like to see my rabbits in their hutches out by the corn crib?" Slade asked.

Thank God Slade's rescuing me. Lissa unclasped her hands from behind her back.

"Take 'em some of them turnip tops, Slade," Aunt Gustie called, sly grin bursting through her wrinkles. "You too, Lissa, air's good for the lungs." Gustie leaned in the doorway, still poking at a back molar, chin softened by her grin.

So they wandered, Stafford, Slade, and Lissa, out to look at the fat rabbits. They grinned and shuffled their feet as they each poked green turnip tops to the bunnies.

"Why, I – Miss Lissa, may I call you Lissa? You know, I've known your folks for years." Stafford turned toward her in his well-tailored black serge suit, broad smile revealing fine white teeth.

Lissa turned, "Why, yes, Reverend Stafford, you may call me Lissa, if you please." *After all, I am of age, past eighteen. But why do I suddenly feel fourteen standing here, bunch of wilted turnip greens in my hands?*

"Good time for an afternoon stroll, isn't it, Lissa? How about it if we took a walk down through that pasture and through those woods? Hickory. Oaks. Lots of yellow and red in the woods. Catch the smell of sassafras." He beamed.

Slade, old enough to see how events were turning, bid good-bye to his rabbits, allowing that he had to tend to Rufus, their dog.

How can one say no to such a powerful man? Lissa stopped herself from digging the toe of her Sunday pump into the soft dust. *It would be like saying no to God.* She hoped he didn't hear her swallow. She brushed back a wisp of hair. *After all, a walk in the woods would work off some of the irritation about Marla Edith and Brandon.* "Why, Reverend Stafford, I'd be pleased to take a walk."

There, she'd said it. She raised her head and joined his stride as his handsome long legs set a healthy pace.

"Now, Lissa, a little request. Like I said, I've known your family for years. Please call me Wardley." You don't have to call me 'Reverend Stafford.'"

"Yes, Reverend – I mean, Wardley." *It, it ... just doesn't seem right. But what can I do?* Lissa's blue dress billowed in the wind, and their feet led them down past the dried-up cattails in the ditch along the split rail fence to the edge of Dodie Creek.

Suddenly Lissa realized that she didn't feel so tight in her chest anymore. Walk was good for her. Balmy day, afternoon graced by billowing white clouds skittering above Baldknob – the yellow sunshine.

"I always appreciate the woods in autumn, Lissa. Is that Virginia Creeper up ahead spreading up that oak?"

"Yes, Reverend St– I mean Wardley, we do have a lot of Virginia Creeper. Don't you think the red leaves on the dogwoods and sassafras are beautiful?"

They chatted, Lissa being sure that she complimented him on his past sermons and the way he'd had the devotions in service today.

"Our church board has interest in ordaining Brandon, doesn't it, Wardley?" Well, Lissa thought that perhaps she shouldn't have brought that subject up, but it had its own way of leaping out.

"Yes, I support it. I favor a fine young man like Brandon. Yes, call of the Lord." Wardley Stafford, a foot taller than Lissa, bowed his greying head and smiled.

"By the way, Lissa." He turned to face her. "That was Miss Marla Edith Maggler at our morning services, wasn't it?" He reached to unhinge a cocklebur that had lodged on his pant's cuff.

Lissa looked up, hoping the annoyance didn't show on her face. "Yes, it was Marla Edith. I expect she heard you were going to preach and came to hear you."

"The Magglers, old friends to my departed Myrna. Marla Edith's father, Sloan, works in the bank now, doesn't he?"

"Yes, he does. He's the loan officer." Lissa's foot slipped on a large burr oak acorn. She lurched sideways.

"My, my, Lissa," his strong hand held her arm, steadying her. "Wouldn't want you to turn a fine ankle like that."

Lissa hoped the conversation would change, the way she felt about Marla Edith these days. His hot fingers bound her arm.

It was cooler in the woods where the path meandered through shadows past old Osage Indian burial mounds.

A stand of persimmon leaned at the edge of Dodie Creek, the leaves, a burgundy mauve. A herd of yellow Guernseys across the fence grazed near the moss-covered footbridge over the creek.

* * *

Gradually the sun slid to the west where golden streaks pierced the sky behind Baldknob. After they had rested on a barkless cottonwood log watching the blackbirds swarm in the cattails over a distant marsh, Lisa suddenly thought of the time. How fast it had gone, and Reverend Stafford had been easy to visit with, after all. She was surprised at his sense of humor. She heard the sound of feet scraping through fallen leaves. Brandon Fall? There he strode, across the fence, stick in his hand, tromping in his work shoes, overall-clad.

"Why, Lissa, surprised to see you here. And Reverend Stafford. Evening."

"Why, good evening, Brandon. What a surprise." Lissa had forgotten the time. Five o'clock already? She looked up at Wardley, who thrust out his chin, now blue with five o'clock shadow, towards the young man across the fence. Hurt twisted around her heart like bindweed around a beanstalk. She struggled for words.

Wardley interrupted. "Yes, what a pleasant surprise, Brandon. My, my, my. Want to tell you again what a fine sermon you had this morning. Isn't that right, Lissa? Three points. Just what they taught me in the preaching class down in the seminary in Memphis." Wardley smiled.

Brandon's feet shifted in his heavy work brogues. Lissa could tell he wondered what she was doing, walking with a fifty-one-year-old man here in the woods.

"Why, thank you, Reverend Stafford. Thank you. I study and do my best. I particularly felt that the Lord was with me today." Brandon cleared his throat.

How lean and tired he looks, Lissa thought. Then she realized that Marla Edith had dropped him off at his place. He'd changed clothes and started after his cows. Lissa had gumption enough to ask him if he and Marla Edith enjoyed their dinner, but she bit her tongue. Was it at Ophelia's? She wanted to ask him how it felt to sit on velvet seats and drive a Buick.

For a moment she could see Marla Edith laughing through her red lips, tossing her hair while forking in the fancy food. Brandon, leaning in, hungry. Who picked up the check? Surely not Brandon

Fall, who'd been considering signing up for the Civilian Conservation Corps?

"Well, good evening, Brandon. Lissa, we'd better head back. I've got a sermon to deliver over at Reeds Spring this evening. Good evening, Brandon."

They turned, the distinguished clergyman, face composed with the satisfaction that the lovely maiden, a schoolteacher, too, had both the courage and good sense to see opportunity when it knocked.

As Lissa turned to accompany the churchman, she heard the Bandon's scarred shoes shuffling through the hickory leaves and brown grass. Brandon trudged along, head lowered. It seemed to Lissa that the soughing grasses whispered her name.

CHAPTER SEVEN

Brandon wrenched his back pitching corn into the ancient corn sheller, which had broken down. Three days passed before he attempted to contact Lissa. He stripped an old canvas jacket over his patched denim shirt, lifted a foot to the ladderback chair to retie his shoe. Maybe I shouldn't even pursue it. Pa and Ma need every ounce of energy and help I can give them now. With the rains stopping, how are we going to make a living? Lissa, she's, well, she deserves....

His heels clonked on the worn wooden steps as he navigated the narrow stairs from his dreary loft room. His mother, Serena, stood by the potbellied stove, a stick of hickory in her thin hand.

Brandon noticed Serena's bent back and realized that her determination to help Pa out of bed in the night was too much for her. Pain shot through his chest at seeing his mother so overburdened and frail.

"Son, you going out this evening?" She smiled, her eyes, clear as morning glories.

Brandon knew she tried to rise above the pain of their circumstances, his father's fall. Three days ago, Owney had dragged himself to the kitchen to drink from the dipper, only to lose his grasp on the doorsill and hit the hard kitchen floor boards.

Serena, out in her garden burning some old weeds and tomato vines, hadn't heard him. It had been thirty minutes before she found him, lying on the floor, chilled, an ugly bruise on his temple.

"Yes, Mother, I need to stretch my legs. Going for a walk through the woods across Dodie Creek. Be back before ten."

Brandon knew she affirmed his interest in scholarly pursuits, and the church reaching out recently gave Serena a real pride which he knew she'd have to check once in a while.

Brandon felt in his coat pocket for the envelope containing his penciled note.

Lissa, meet me tomorrow night by the footbridge over Dodie Creek at eight o'clock.

He wanted to write more but hesitated when he realized it implied, "We need to talk." Would he have the courage to say what his heart wanted to say? How could he ask her, submerged as they were in such blighting poverty?

Brandon thought of the letter his Aunt Beulah sent from somewhere on lonely Route 66, headed for California.

We had to eat wild greens since January this year. Violet tops, wild onions, forget-me-nots, wild lettuce, and such weeds cows eat. Our family is in bad shape, children need milk, women need nourishment, food, shoes, dresses.

Their hearts ached with the stark pain of it, the reality of it. Brandon wished the battery hadn't conked out on their tinny radio, so he could hear President Roosevelt explain the New Deal and the WPA.

An owl hooted. A half moon provided enough light for his steps as he tromped through the stand of post oak toward Dodie Creek bridge. Stark realities of the drought were muted by the silver moonlight. An owl hooted.

Somewhere over west a coyote called. The yellow and brown oak leaves crinkled beneath his feet. Spicy smells of walnut and wood smoke filled his nostrils. A wind sweeping over Iron Mountain blew a tangy breath. The last of the tree frogs chirped at the twinkling stars overhead. In spite of his back ache and burdens, Brandon Fall recognized "The Lord is at hand."

As he picked up his stride through the meadow on the other side of Dodie Creek, a silver grey possum waddled across his path, heading for the persimmon tree. He could see the moonlight dancing off the tin roof of Lissa's Blue Vale schoolhouse ahead, beneath the sycamores and elm. He thought about how unfortunate it was, Marla Edith accusing Lissa of stealing her school. What were the details, anyway? Maybe Lissa could explain it more and the two of them could come to a truce.

When he reached the school, Brandon dug in his pocket for his envelope and note. Carefully, he slid it under the unpainted door, rust-streaked from the hinges. She'd find it first thing in the morning. He headed toward the longer path through Violet Vale, and over Buzzard Hill, feet rustling through the dry grass toward home. Tomorrow night, yes, Lissa and I must talk.

* * *

It'd been a fine day at Blue Vale School. Lissa, in her violet pleated shirtwaist dress, bent over Tippy Mae Maggler's desk to praise her. Today, Tippy Mae said her five multiplication tables all the way to five-times-twelve without missing a single one. Lissa hoped the tables wouldn't slip through her head in a few days, lackluster as Tippy Mae could be.

Eileen Storm grinned at Lissa through her uneven teeth, which she'd remembered to brush with soda and salt that morning, as they were too poor to buy toothpaste. She'd handed Lissa her mother's last red rose.

Lissa placed it in a small glass bottle and set it on the organ by the blackboard.

Sunlight bounced off the walls of the otherwise dreary schoolroom, the rays fracturing on the glass vase holding the wild asters and goldenrod Lissa had found by a little spring where water still trickled.

Even Orbert and Elroy Terfer hadn't had their squabble at recess, elbowing each other, struggling over who got the biggest nubbin apple from their lunch pail.

A warmth crept through her as she glanced again at the note,

Lissa, meet me tomorrow night by the footbridge over Dodie Creek at eight o'clock.

She smiled, and her heart felt light as a feather, buoyed by a gentle breeze. Sure. She'd go. After supper, and after she graded the geography tests and Needa Hodge's essay on the 4-H Club. She realized she was blushing as she suddenly remembered the brush of Brandon's warm lips on her cheek.

That second point in Brandon's Sunday sermon, "Let your moderation be known in all things," flashed through Lissa's mind. Even now in the schoolroom she could hear his mellow voice.

* * *

Estra greeted Lissa by the pitcher pump that evening, broad smile on her face. "Why, Lissa. Good news. You know those old hens, eating nothing but grasshoppers this year? Well, Harris Hobson drove out from Slavanski's Produce over in Branson. Buying up old hens."

Lissa stared at her mother. Now what? Brandon's note. *Meet me at eight o'clock.* She started to speak, but Estra continued. "Paid me thirty cents a piece, Lissa. You know those old hens mostly stopped laying, anyway."

Lissa reached for a water tumbler to get herself a drink from the pitcher pump as her mother continued.

"You know what we have to do tonight when the pullets go to roost, Lissa, move them from the brooder house into the empty hen house."

No. Not tonight, Lissa wanted to say, but she bit her tongue. Maybe. Maybe if we hurry. How long did it take us last year?

"Took us three hours last year, but that was on account of the downpour and the mud balling up on our shoes like it did. This year...." Estra didn't finish her sentence.

To make matters worse, Lissa had forgotten Clementine's sore teat where she'd snagged it on barbed wire last week. Her fingers squeezed it too hard during milking, and Clementine hiked her right hind leg and kicked backwards, the foot clunking down into Lissa's half-full milk pail, crumpling the pail and spilling the milk.

Lissa had to run to the milkhouse to find another pail and check her anger at Clementine.

She had to let her papers go, in order to get to the brooder house near the plum thicket by seven o'clock. "That's it, Slade. Grab the pullets by the leg with the wire hook," Lissa encouraged.

Slade, batting the choking dust and flying feathers, reached out with the snag wire to hook a protesting Leghorn pullet. "How many did you say you can carry, Lissa?"

"Three in each hand. Need two more, Slade." Lissa coughed as she breathed the dust and feathers.

"I can take four, Slade." Estra smiled, head bound in her old grey scarf, her patched apron spread across her dress. Estra's voice reflected her triumph in selling the old hens at such a good price, in hard times, too.

Tromp, tromp. Back and forth. Lissa bit her lip, three squawking pullets flapping in each hand. She had forgotten how heavy they were. When she reached the henhouse a hundred yards away, she pried open the door with a scarred shoe toe and tossed in the bewildered pullets.

"There. New home. You'll get used to it in about a week. Stop squawking." Lissa recognized that there was an edge to her voice and that the pullets weren't at fault.

She turned, trotting back up the path to the brooder house, stepping aside for Estra, bent over with her four flapping pullets, dangling by the legs in her hands. Lissa slid past the dead maple leaning starkly in the moonlight, as a ghostly cloud hovered at the edge of the half-moon.

"Why, Lissa, we'll be done in no time at all." Slade, amidst his choking, tried to encourage his fatigued sister.

"How many more, Slade?" The squawking chickens rattled Lissa's brains, as by now the pullets were awake and all were clucking nervously.

"I'd say about a hundred." He coughed, then sneezed, which slowed him further.

"Let me take the wire, Slade, you carry pullets a while." But Lissa discovered she wasn't as crafty with the hooked wire as her brother and had to hand it back.

A blustering wind came up, making it difficult to open the brooder house door without it slapping back, allowing three or four frightened pullets to escape and fly high over Lissa's head, aiming for the low branch of the dead maple. The strong headwind slowed Estra and Lissa as they tromped heavily towards the henhouse. It seemed a mile away. Now the cloud conspired and covered the half-moon. Lissa stumbled over a dead limb that had fallen over the path. One pullet jerked loose from her left hand and flew for the plum thicket on the right.

A queston surged in Lissa's mind. Was there anything really wrong with Marla Edith's Buick that Sunday? Engine trouble, is that how she got him out there? What was Marla Edith doing in our church, anyway? The Magglers left years ago for the town church. A suffocating feeling weighed on Lissa's chest, and the canned beef she'd had for supper clustered in a knot in her stomach. That's what I want to talk to Brandon about. How could he drive off with her in that Buick of her dad's? But just could it be something else? Asking her to....

"Only about fifty pullets left," Slade called, proud of their achievement. Lissa slammed the flimsy brooder house door and staggered back toward the henhouse. This time Reverend Stafford's face caught in her mind. "Just call me Wardley," he'd said, smiling with those curved, masculine lips. How old was he, anyway? Well, not every girl her age had the opportunity to take an afternoon stroll on a fine autumn day with such a churchman. Widower or not.

Lissa wondered what was the matter with her. Her cheeks felt hot when she remembered Brandon and the note. She heard the rumble of a car and noticed lights bouncing off the hedge trees along the lane. Her arms ached from the weight of the chickens. "Who would be driving up our lane tonight? Looks like a new car.

Lissa tossed the chickens through the henhouse door, twisted the latch, then hurried to the edge of the front yard to see if she could recognize the car. Another worry flooded her mind. Brandon. I'll be late. Then she remembered she hadn't told her mother about his note. The car, evidently driven by someone who was lost, halted by the barn for a moment. Then it made a circle by the corn crib and roared back out the lane. Lissa caught a glimpse of it purring down the hedge row. Someone from town lost in these hills. Only city people had new cars that purred like that. It did look like the Maggler car, didn't it? But it couldn't be Marla Edith, she knows where we live.

* * *

A quarter to eight? I'm going to be late. Lissa let the soiled dress fall at her feet as she kicked her scuffed shoes to the side, stockings falling over them.

"So far I haven't felt any chicken mites crawling around," Lissa mumbled as she slopped water into the basin on her wash stand and splashed her face and her arms. No time for a full bath.

"Oh, my hair." Lissa gasped as she glimpsed her frowzy hair, feathers dotting it here and there. She grabbed her hair brush and raked through it. Oh, well, it's night. Important thing is to be there. No time to take my hair down now.

She struggled into a blue sweater and headed for the stairs, hoping that the lily of the valley toilet water masked the chicken smell. "Mother, I'm going for a walk."

Lissa didn't even bother to turn and face her mother as she raced through the dining room door and out onto the wide porch.

"Late as it is? Don't you have papers to grade?" Estra's eyes opened wide.

"Got to have fresh air, Mother, after choking on chicken feathers." Lissa realized that her mother would allow that that made sense.

Lissa raced through the barnyard to the gate. Her fingers fidgeted. Where is the latch? To make matters worse, their four milk cows lay belching their cud, sullenly, wedged against the gate.

"Up, get up...." Lissa called out as the nighthawk gave a piercing cry.

Her shoes hit the hard path across the pasture she and Wardley Stafford had taken only days ago. Now Lissa had another goal. Brandon Fall. Will I ask him what he had to eat over in Springfield? Did Marla Edith remember her manners, or did she fork in lamb, or was it salmon, or fried chicken, like she did at the pie supper with

Wolfgang Hotter?

Lissa checked herself. No, I don't want to meet Brandon when I'm angry. Let your moderation....

The cloud bank slid past the half-moon, making it easier for Lissa to see the path where it fell along Dodie Creek. Late in the season, she didn't have to worry about copperheads. Her shoes pounded the path. Up ahead she could see the towering walnut next to the old mulberry with the wide limb where she and Brandon had sat when they were children. A horned owl called, "Whooo, whooo."

The soles of her shoes hit the footbridge planks. The boards shuddered. She'd forgotten the bridge was so old and shaky. There. Up ahead. Brandon? By the mulberry?

Lissa had forgotten her wrist watch, but she guessed that it was at least eight thirty. One lone frog chirped what seemed to be "too late, too late." No, that wasn't Brandon up ahead, it was only a shadow from a wild rose bush.

The twisted, low-hanging mulberry limb reached out toward her. Moonlight glanced off the rough bark. A lonely wind whistled through the bridge railings. Stars winked from an indigo sky. A whippoorwill called, but there was no answering call. Where was Brandon?

Lissa sat on the wide limb as the night wind cooled the sweat on her brow. She waited until she was ashamed to wait any longer. Her leg grew numb from the pinching bark.

"He came, but since I was late, he thought I didn't want to meet him anymore," she whispered.

Lissa, chin sinking toward her breast, meandered down the hard clay path of the short cut through the Johnson grass toward home, a hand resting on the small of her aching back.

CHAPTER EIGHT

The autumn days drifted into a crisp November, yet by midday, the sun had melted the frost, warming the air to a mellow Indian Summer.

Brandon bent over the sawhorse on Marla Edith Maggler's back porch. His weathered hand grasped the plank as his right arm brought the ripsaw across the penciled line.

Marla Edith, in her turquoise skirt and sweater, shiny hair poked into a matching snood, stood on a flagstone below. Her dark eyes focused on Brandon's easy masculine movements. Pink lipstick, complementing the turquoise, highlighted her ample lips.

Brandon felt his broad shoulders stretch in the faded denim shirt as he lifted the board, his patched jacket draped on the porch railing, sweat beads at the hairline on his brow.

"Here, Brandon, let me steady that board for you." Marla Edith reached to clasp the end of the seven-foot yellow pine board he stretched across the sawhorse, while taking note of the strength in his hand and arm, even if he was thin as a prairie poplar. The sawing motions shook the board. Brandon gripped the plank more firmly. Marla Edith stretched for a closer grasp. Her hand brushed his. Brandon, feeling the heat of her olive-tinted flesh, shifted a foot encased in a heavy work shoe and cleared his throat.

Sensible thing to take this job. Seventy-five cents a day? Where else could I make that kind of money?

What had added to his misery was the second fall his pa, Owney, had taken a week ago. He'd failed to obey Serena's direction. "Owney, don't you try to walk across the floor until I'm in here to help you. You just call me."

But hearing their dog, Yippi, barking near the barn, Owney ignored Serena's instruction. He'd struggled to his feet, grabbed his crutch, and dragged himself toward the porch door.

Just what they needed, another setback. Pa lying there even longer than the time before – breaking his paralyzed arm in two places.

"We can drive into Branson to the Red Onion Cafe for lunch. They have roast beef every Saturday," Marla Edith said as she nudged his shoulder with the butt of her hand.

Since Brandon's mind had drifted, she repeated the suggestion, adding, "And if we have time, we can stroll over to the Rexall for an ice cream soda."

Brandon lifted the plank and held it up to the framework enclosing the porch. He turned, lifting sad brown eyes to hers. "Brought my own lunch. Put it over there with my coat by the post." He realized that the egg-and-biscuit sandwich would be measly and insufficient, only announcing his poverty. He was ravenous already. *Am I getting in deeper? How does Marla Edith take all this, the time I'm spending here?* Yet, Brandon didn't want to be rude. "We'll see," he said, picking up his hammer and slipping two nails into his mouth.

Eighty-seven-dollar hospital bill. The painful events weighed like rocks inside him. How long had it taken him to start up the Model T? Forty, fifty turns of the crank?

His shoulder still ached. Loading Ma Serena, and Pa, hunched, chilling from pain. They'd chugged off for the hospital at Ozark, knowing the gas was low in the tank.

"I believe he's going into shock," Serena had said, "Won't it go faster?"

The shuddering car came to a halt only fifty feet up Buzzard Hill.

"Now, what'll we do?" Tears streamed down Serena's lined cheeks.

"Going to have to turn her around and try to back up," Brandon replied as Mother Poverty grinned again.

He had managed it. But it was the pitifulness of it. The Buzzard Hill incline proved too steep and the gas, low and sloshing backwards in the tank, couldn't trickle down to the carburetor. Only by turning the tinny Ford around and backing up the steep hill had he been able to reach the crest.

With the radiator boiling, they chugged on toward Ozark. That's when they'd met Marla Edith streaming toward them in her father's Buick. He'd flagged her down and called out, "You headed out toward Watson's Store, Marla Edith?"

"Why, yes, I'm on my way home, Brandon. Trouble? Anything I can do?"

"Taking Pa to the hospital. Believe he's broken his arm. Marla Edith, could I ask you to do me a favor? Could you drive by the Massey house and tell Lissa I can't meet her tonight?" Discouragement surged through Brandon's heart as he thought of missing Lissa. Shame that he was so poor as to have to involve Marla Edith as a message bearer.

Marla had agreed to spread the word and roared off in the Buick in the dark, taillights glowing. Since then Lissa had been so distant. Why? Even at church she had that eyes-cast-down look, and at times she seemed to avoid him when he'd tried to tell her about the night of their troubles. But that was part of it, his family and their troubles. Too many challenges and burdens. Didn't the Masseys have enough of their own? Besides, who was he to even think about a proposal of marriage to anyone, times like they were?

They'd made it to the hospital with Owney. Took thirty extra minutes, all the time Pa shivering from shock. Three days at Mercy Hospital – bill of eighty-seven dollars. Brandon recognized that shoving the Springfield Bible College class schedule to the back of his desk had been the appropriate thing to do. No school now.

He was brought back to the present when he felt Marla Edith's soft arm brush his as she reached to steady the board he nailed at the top two-by-four.

Around ten o'clock, she poured him a cup of steaming coffee. They sat on the wide back porch steps facing the sloping yard, and tree-lined pasture beyond. A cow mooed. A meadowlark perched on the fence, stretched its yellow throat, and poured out a song. Drifts from the sweet alfalfa filled the air.

"Isn't it interesting," Marla Edith said, shaking her hair bagged in her snood, "Lissa Massey and that widower, Wardley Stafford, attending services together over at Reeds Spring?" Her brown eyes lingered on his, checking his reaction.

Brandon felt as though he was struggling alone across Death Valley. Her words swirled in his head, in his heart, in his chest, in his bones. The poverty, the out-of-controllness of it all. The fatigue. The insufficient food. How long had they eaten poke and dandelion greens last spring? Until they'd no longer been able to endure the bitterness. He was so sick of turnips this fall that the smell made him gag.

Well, understandable. "Reverend Stafford's a fine man. A fine man," he said. Brandon braced himself to rise and begin with the two-by-four. He would not criticize Lissa in front of anyone. Certainly not in front of Marla Edith, who still seemed boiling over the Blue Vale School situation.

How can I blame her? I know Lissa waited. Waited alone in the darkness for me. What can I offer her now? Stafford? Yes, he's older, but he has station in life, security. Didn't all the women adore Wardley Stafford? Lissa has a right to the things I can't provide her. Brandon couldn't stop the thoughts.

The fire station siren in Branson wailed twelve o'clock. The noontime autumn sun and crisp air increased the hunger gnawing at his gut.

"Time to stop. Pa's not needing the Buick today, Brandon. Need a change. Let me grab my purse, I can smell that roast beef already, gravy, potatoes." Her ample breast brushed his shoulder as she leaped, more heavily than she'd intended, to her feet. "Let me trot in and slip into my pumps."

What would Marla Edith be without her high-heeled pumps? Brandon smiled to himself. Starved as he was, he poked in the biscuit and egg while she was inside primping herself for lunch in town.

Maybe driving the Buick would lift his depression. Besides, he needed to check at the hardware store for some more ten-penny nails.

The satin feel of the steering wheel, the easy rumble of the powerful motor, and the Buick's glittering hood ornament ahead, all had their way of causing Brandon's blood to surge more rapidly. Besides, he could smell the Evening in Paris Marla had splashed on her neck.

"You have to tell me about the deacons of your church, Brandon, and how they plan to get you ready to be a minister. Preaching again this coming Sunday, aren't you?" Marla Edith stretched her arm across the back of the plush seat, her fingers toying with the brown curls at his neck.

Brandon stiffened at the touch of her fingers above his shirt collar.

Ahead, the brick streets of Branson – town of eight hundred, founded as a logging town after the railroad shot through, spread on the banks of White River. The white spire of the Congregational Church rose above the red oaks surrounding it. Trumpet vines folks had planted in yards and by fences swayed starkly, minus their orange blossoms.

A few Saturday shoppers dragged along the sidewalks, eyeing lean merchandise in sparsely dressed windows. Who had money these days, since the stock market crash?

The front end of the Buick swayed and rocked opulently as it was designed to do, mounted on heavy springs. Brandon braked and eased it into a parking space between a wreck of a Chevrolet and a Model A truck with a broken window.

He reached for the door handle, aware that Marla Edith waited on the plush seat for him to step around and open her door. Her ear bobs sparkled in the light.

Well, gentleman thing to do. He caught the drift of her heavy perfume as Marla Edith reached for his arm, lifted her leg sheathed in silk hose, and slid out.

No sooner had their shoes touched the edge of the sidewalk, when Bart Maggler, face shadowed by a three-day stubble, loped along, hands shoved into his hip pockets, which caused his coattail to wag between his hands. Tippy Mae rolled along a pace behind, penny lollipop dangling from the corner of her mouth. Her dirty hair ribbon had come loose, and her fat braid had started to unravel. Her eyes opened wide as she removed her sucker to holler, "Why, Aunt Marla

Edith, you comin in to town with Miss Massey's boyfriend?" Tippy Mae's face fell in shock, taking it in.

Marla Edith clasped the hard muscle in Brandon's arm and glared at her niece, Tippy Mae. "Speak when spoken to. Don't you have any manners at all?" She hurried past the forlorn girl. Her left high heel turned beneath her, but she regained her stride.

Red Onion diners turned their heads to stare at Miss Maggler and her tall carpenter friend. The manager, Tolbert Hollister, straightened his wire-rimmed glasses and raked his palm over his bald head as Miss Marla Edith Maggler bounced toward his best table by the window. Brandon hoped his face wasn't red as he remembered to reach out and draw out the ladder-back chair.

Old man Bittikoffer and Elim Goshel put down their forks in order to appreciate Miss Maggler showing them how a *real* lady walks in high heels.

Edith Wharton and her husband, Sam, who attended the Full Gospel Church, turned to stare at the couple. "Well, Marla Edith Maggler's hooked her claws into Lissa Massey's man, ain't she?" whispered Edith, straightening her faded winter hat.

"Well, he ain't gonna git to no seminary, messin round with them Magglers," she rasped to Sam.

CHAPTER NINE

"Get that dried-up old cedar tree out of the front room," Aunt Gustie ordered, her white hair grinning beneath the edges of her new dust cap made from a red beet-patterned scrap of feed sack, apron to match.
"Yes, it's over. Christmas is over. Tree's shedding on the rug. Slade, let's strip off the decorations." Lissa realized her mind was whirling. How can I stop the thoughts? Why am I irritated when I think of Brandon? Am I too responsive to Wardley Stafford's affections? Where is all of this leading? Why does Brandon look so hangdog and seem to avoid me? Lissa admitted that as she thought of her dignified and charming churchman friend, she warmed inside and could feel a smile creeping over her lips.
"I'll pull off the popcorn strands," Slade said. Lissa admitted that the past week had been a happy Christmas time, in spite of the absence of their father, Jessee.
"We can throw it out for the chickens." Slade pulled and gathered at the string of popcorn. "Sure do thank you for the book, Lissa, I've always wanted *Wild Animals I Have Known*."
"You're welcome, Slade." Lissa wondered if Slade noticed what she was feeling, the tornness.
Lissa removed the dozen small, old glass globe ornaments. No money for extra tree decorations. Considering the hard times, she'd felt blessed at Christmas. Blessed and torn.
But that's life, wasn't it? Blessings and tornness. New people.

New relationships. New opportunities, and the losses. At least, that was the way she looked at it.

Lissa covered the ornaments with cotton batting, then started to pick off the tinfoil icicles. Even though the tree, cut from the wild cedars growing along the pasture fence, still smelled fragrant, it was dangerously dry and needed to be tossed out by the woodpile where Slade could cut it up for kindling.

Aunt Gustie tromped across the dining room threshold, clonking her heels on the wide planks between the linoleum and the rug. "I'd say you done right well, Lissa, that amber necklace Reverend Stafford give you."

Lissa glanced at her old aunt and wondered if the remark was intended as a dig to irritate her. *Am I too touchy these days?*

"Yes, Aunt Gustie. It's nice, and I'm fond of it." Lissa thought of her surprise when she started to get out of the Essex and Wardley had handed her the little coffin-like box with the oval-shaped piece of amber on a gold-toned chain coiled inside.

Well, it wasn't a sapphire, or a ruby, and Lissa doubted if the chain was fourteen-carat gold. Surely not too expensive. Yet – her mind drifted as a pleasant warmth crept through her. A year full of sorrows. The struggle of getting started at Blue Vale School. Marla Edith's slurs. Brandon's confusing withdrawal. The drought and the financial crisis stirring havoc everywhere.

Lissa had to admit Wardley Stafford's small gift softened the rough edges of life, and the touch of his well-manicured fingers on hers brought comfort. She had purchased a leather billfold for Brandon, but that was before he left her stranded at Dodie Creek Bridge. It lay in its wrapping on her bureau as she waited for an opportunity to give it to someone. Give it to Wardley? Lissa felt guilty, too, for sometimes thinking it would be easier if Brandon did join the Civilian Conservation Corps. When she saw him at services lately, she tried to wait for him, at least have a short conversation. But then she could see folks cornering him about his sermon. The other thing, Brandon being so tied up late fall even into the Christmas season over at the Magglers'. It seemed like building that office room for Marla Edith went on forever. And just what was *that* relationship?

"I take it as a good thing, Marla Edith hiring Brandon that way." Aunt Gustie coughed as she stepped back into the room. "Seventy-five cents a day is better wages than a feller can get anywhere these days."

"You're right, Aunt Gustie. Brandon had the extra burden of that hospital bill after his father broke his arm. I'm glad too. People ruining their backs chopping cotton last season down in Arkansas for fifty cents a day." But a part of her wanted to say, Isn't he being taken in? He's not dating Marla Edith, yet she takes him everywhere since his Model T looks like it's ready for Boyd Beemer's junk yard, cords grinning through the tires, roof leaking, fenders rusting. How does Marla Edith interpret it, hovering over him like she does?

"And," continued Aunt Gustie, grabbing the broom to sweep up the dried bits of cedar, "If Brandon's interested in being a real preacher, ain't it contradictory to be spending all that time with the Magglers?" Gustie's eyes rolled up as if pleased she'd used a big word like *contradictory*. "Marla Edith coming over to White Oak church, now, isn't she?" Gustie stared at Lissa.

Estra stepped into the room. "Didn't we have a nice Christmas? Couldn't you just feel your dear father's presence? I keep thinking of Brandon's last point in that sermon, 'The Lord is at hand.'"

"Yes, Mother. I do still feel Father's presence. I'll always feel his influence in my life." Lissa swallowed. Why did she have to mention Brandon? In spite of the tears in her eyes, still she was glad they could talk about her father's death these days without such raw pain.

"Deacon Whitsitt told me after Sunday school last week," Estra continued as she tucked in the edges of the throw she had draped over their only stuffed chair, "that the church board proposes to ordain Brandon soon. Sometime in February."

"We all knew that'd happen. How could White Oak Church pass up a candidate like Brandon? He'll get his seminary training when the times are better, you'll see." Lissa wanted to be registered with those who believed in Brandon Fall and his call to the ministry, even though she knew he was avoiding her.

"Then too, Lissa, you know our own Reva Rennart is engaged to that St. Mark seminary student, Elwin Nevins, up in Kansas City. Guess Reva and Elwin will settle for city living, if he can get a church there."

Lissa thought of auburn-headed Reva, struggling on the hog farm with her parents and two brothers. How recently, Reva had taken a part-time job in Branson caring for bedfast old Sarah Parrish.

"And Lissa, you'll be going with Reverend Stafford for his Faith and Life lectures at the Stone Church up in Springfield. That's tomorrow, isn't it?"

Lissa realized her mother just couldn't bring herself to call the distinguished elder "Wardley." "Yes, it is, Mother, last day of my vacation, except Sunday. Then back to the scholars at Blue Vale."

But that was a good thing. The scholars. The fun of it. Hard work, but always something new to be discovered. First grader, Andy Shotts, learning to read. Mary Sue Everlot singing *The First Noel* while she played the pump organ at the Christmas program. And how the folks congratulated both her and the students.

Lissa thought of their little gifts to her, a jar of plum preserves, a hand-carved letter opener. A box of home-made divinity, and most of all, their smiles, their love as they had crowded around her, hearts thumping as she opened the gifts.

Lissa realized that life was composed of little things. Life lay deepest in the little things.

* * *

Radiant shafts of sunlight beamed through the pines and the cedars along the curving blacktop road leading to Springfield. Lissa had debated whether or not she should go with Wardley. Yet Deacon Whitsitt had said it'd be a fine thing to have a representative in person from White Oak Church at the conference – bring back a report of the meetings. "Yes, a schoolmom's the best person for that job," Brother Whitsitt had assured her.

Lissa had worn her tan winter coat with the brown bear fur collar, more like a shawl, across her shoulders. She'd checked her seams to see if they ran straight, slipped into her brown pumps, though they were not as high-heeled as Marla Edith's. She settled her brown hat she had ordered from Sears Roebuck and Company at a slant on her tightly-pinned hair. The saucy feather angled upward.

"Wonderful how the Lord leads, Lissa. Just wonderful. See how he provided that carpenter job over at Maggler's for Brandon?" Wardley turned to her and smiled.

Lissa glanced over at Wardley's powerful hands gripping the Essex's wheel as he maneuvered the corner by a gnarled hackberry, branches black against a cold blue sky, a flock of blackbirds scattering.

How distinguished Wardley looked in his black homburg. Her father had never been able to afford a hat like that. Just a simple grey fedora.

"Yes, I have to wonder, sometimes, Wardley, how one knows the Lord is leading." Should I tell him about Blue Vale and how Marla Edith tells everyone I stole her school? And my anxiety about the activity day contest coming up? My confusion about Brandon? Lissa decided she would hold her tongue.

"Only say kind things about others," Estra often told her. "Remember, those things are in the Lord's hands."

Wardley steered the Essex up to the curb in front of the high-roofed stone church, parking it in a space marked "Clergy." Before he unlatched the car door, he glanced again at Lissa. Then he seemed to forget himself and the time as his eyes surveyed Lissa, her face, her petite body in well-chosen clothes.

Lissa, aware that Wardley seemed momentarily captivated by her, felt a tinge of uneasiness sweep over her, yet a pride, too. Young woman like her accompanying such a learned man. Youthful looking at his age. Lissa just wished the ladies in the sewing circle wouldn't tease her so much about it, even though she knew those women took more than an ordinary interest in her and the growing relationship with Stafford.

"Have you ever seen the oak staircase in his house in Branson?" Lottie Links asked, lifting her brown eyes from tiny quilt stitches.

"Seven rooms in that house. Bedrooms upstairs and down. And, Lissa, a *bathroom*." Celeste Simmons cleared her throat and stared straight at Lissa. "Think what that means, Lissa, no hightailing it out to the privy on a winter night."

"What ever happened to you and Brandon Fall?" Roma Salzer queried. "I always thought Brandon Fall's about the best man there is for a young lady in these parts."

Well, she'd had to listen and make polite replies as best she could, knowing the ladies meant no harm and were trying to encourage what they considered a good thing. Lissa concluded that Brandon Fall was his own man in his own right. In the proper time, after his ordination in the church, regular pay check, and President Roosevelt's New Deal lifting everyone and everything up, Brandon might then have some very important matters to discuss with her.

I mustn't get in the way. Wait for the Lord in spite of the sadness inside, she decided.

* * *

Wardley's lectures at the Faith and Life conference lifted Lissa's spirits. A major point dealt with the necessity for larger churches like theirs to secure seminary-trained pastors. Reva's fiancé, Elwin Nevins, for instance. But everyone knew Elwin opted for a city church. He'd never come to White Oak. The old ways of ordaining untrained people for the clergy were passing. That is, except for Brandon Fall. Besides, he did plan to go to seminary.

Lissa found it easy to sit with the delegates and listen to such a polished speaker as Wardley. His mellow voice and cultured enunciations eased a tired place, deep within her heart. She had to admit that what several of the women delegates whispered was indeed true, "Widower Stafford is handsome."

* * *

Wardley turned the Essex's long hood into Lissa's lane as the car rocked up toward the Massey house, grey roof reflecting the moonlight, dim light downstairs in the living room, lamps lit in the upstairs bedrooms.

"Sorry I got you back so late, Lissa. Must be after nine. But you ought to get a good night's rest before church services tomorrow."

"It's all right, Wardley. I'm really not that tired, and the conference refreshed me. Your knowledge about the Apostle Paul, his devotion and commitment, helped me."

The car pulled to a stop before the slatted gate by the flagstone walk leading to the porch.

"Wardley, wouldn't you like to come in for a cup of tea?" After all, she thought it would be bad manners not to invite him in. "Mother left a lamp lit for me."

"Why, Lissa. Yes. Some other things I do want to talk over with you. You being such an *important* friend to me, especially since the Lord took dear Myrna...." His voice faded as he opened his door, long legs carrying him around the back of the car to open Lissa's door.

Before Lissa stepped out to the kitchen, she stopped at the stand table in the dining room to turn on the dial of their Philco radio, shaped like a cathedral window. Thankful that last week Estra had surprised them by taking five dollars of her old hen money to buy the family a new radio battery, Lissa adjusted the dial as the sweet sounds of Paul Whitman's Orchestra flooded into the living room.

The Seth Thomas clock on the east wall shelf struck ten. Wardley sat in the hard oak rocker, stretching his legs sheathed in navy serge, feet resting on the roses in the oval hooked rug before him.

Lissa poked up the fire in the kitchen range with the poker. In a few minutes, steam hissed from the the cast-iron teakettle. Sweetness from her mother's bouquet of dried sage, rosemary, and cedar drifted through the rooms.

"It's orange pekoe tea, Wardley, and I've brought along some of the coconut macaroons Mother made yesterday."

Lissa set the tray on the library table, poured hot tea into the green cups with the pink rosebuds on the sides. She handed the first cup to Wardley. Turning, she took a cookie and seated herself four feet in front of him at the edge of the leather and oak couch.

"My, cozy here in this country home, Lissa. Yes." Wardley sipped his tea.

Maybe he wants to tell me something about Brandon's ordination plans, Lissa thought.

The small talk continued. Would it be quite so nice tomorrow, or was that a storm front over Inspiration Point bringing in some sleet? Had they been able to salvage any corn this year, with the drought? Lissa would soon be preparing her scholars for the spring activity day over in Ozark, wouldn't she? Wasn't it nice, Reva Rennart's fiancé in his last seminary year up there at St. Mark seminary? Only when she'd taken his empty cup, setting it back on the tray, had he risen. Tall, broad-shouldered, handsome in his fifty-one years as he stood in the soft lamplight, Wardley cleared his throat, and his dark eyes looked as though they were filled with the longing of Jacob waiting for the seven years to pass.

"Lissa, Lissa, there is something...." Wardley's voice lowered as he reached forward. Lissa, standing before him, thought she should offer to get his overcoat. She glanced up attentively, open to the distinguished man looking at her so kindly.

"Lissa, why, I must be direct about this." His well-manicured hand clasped her slender yielding one. "Lissa, my dear, I have something important to ask you." Wardley's other strong hand reached gently around her back as he looked intensely into her blue eyes.

"Lissa, I love you, and I'm asking you to marry me. It's been three years now since Myrna...."

Lissa's heart skipped. For a moment she closed her eyes as a dizziness hit her. The surprise of it. Affection. Warmth for him. Great respect. But not this. Marry? Her neck felt hot.

Lissa didn't hear the rest of the sentence. She realized she was staring at him, yet she didn't pull her hand from his large warm one. A part of her acknowledged the comfort and security of his broad chest and throbbing hand.

Wardley drew her closer, bent his Clark Gable face to Lissa's, his curved lips kissing hers.

CHAPTER TEN

"Gee, I think that's just swell, Lissa, and I hear Reverend Stafford's going to trade the Essex off on a new Olds. Think of it, Lissa, an *Olds*!"

Lissa was glad Slade hadn't openly disapproved of her engagement to Wardley Stafford, though she'd seen him try to hide his fallen face. She knew it was because of Brandon's drop from their world – except at church. But even that was different. Lissa realized that this wasn't the time, but she simply must caution Slade not to use those vulgar words creeping in these modern times – swell, slick chick, oomph girl, meat ball – what were the others?

Brandon's eyes had a haunted look as he'd stood behind the pulpit last week. Lissa was certain that his call to the ministry was deep and urgent and that he gave himself fully in response. She shouldn't get in his way. She thought of President Roosevelt and his fireside chats on the Philco, how he used the best English, encouraging everyone in the country not to give up hope, that "all we have to fear is fear itself."

Lissa concluded that had been true for her, too, hadn't it? Finally catching her breath, she had sorted out her answer to Wardley Stafford's question that had made her dizzy. Dizzy, not sick.

"I'll bet that high-up Preacher Stafford broke out with the hives, waitin' them four days till you sorted it out and come to a conclusion," Aunt Gustie said, sporting a white dust cap this time.

"I knew it was coming," said Estra, taking Lissa's warm hand in hers, gentle smile on her lips. "He's a fine man, Reverend Stafford. Just think, the station you'll have in life...."

"Station? Station, my foot," scoffed Aunt Gustie. "Only station is the Missouri Pacific in Branson, and I think it's gonna close." Her coarse laugh rose.

"Mother, I-I ... I just don't know. Well, a part of me knows. It isn't that I don't have feelings for Wardley, it's ... well, you know our ages." Lissa's blue eyes searched her mother's face.

"You'll know, Lissa. Neither I nor anyone else can advise you. It must come from your heart, your answer."

They sat, just the two of them, since Aunt Gustie had decided to hike back to her cabin for a pint of sorghum molasses. The morning light broke through the kitchen window as they sipped the hot tea while the teakettle hissed on the wood range behind them. The sweet aroma of navy beans simmering with smoked ham hocks filled the room.

Last night's dream flooded Lissa's mind, a visit with her old pal Millie Millsap, who had moved over the Ozark Mountains to Batesville, Arkansas, with her widowed father to take up work in the casket factory.

Lissa wished Millie was with her now. But hadn't Millie been there in the dream? Her natural brown curls encircling Millie's freckled face as they walked leisurely along the road leading to Lit Watson's store? Like the two travelers on the Emmaus road, they had dialogued it.

"Shall I marry him, Millie?"

Millie smiled, touched her shoulder and said, "Lissa, remember, we don't always seize our opportunities."

What made it so serious was the fact that the dream repeated itself two more times, each time Millie saying to her, "Remember, we don't always seize our opportunities."

Well, before Lissa left her room this morning, she'd written Millie a short letter about Wardley's proposal and the comforting dream.

Brandon? The Lord's leading? It seemed clear to Lissa that the Lord had given Brandon his own craggy path, his own challenges like John the Baptist, or old Elijah. Brandon, even taking on some of the lean intensity of a prophet, his spirit, tempered by the tasks before him, didn't seem to include marriage.

And Aunt Gustie? "Well, I declare. Hee, hee hee," she cackled. "In the days of George Washington and Thomas Jefferson, them old goats married young wives. Yep."

Lissa remembered how she waited for Aunt Gustie to finish. It hadn't been so bad at all – mostly teasing.

"Why, Lissa, you know Wardley Stafford's plenty young enough to father children. Plenty young," Gustie had emphasized, glazed look in her eyes.

Lissa loved her Aunt Gustie and even had given her five dollars for Christmas to add to her savings for the false teeth she planned on buying sometime this year.

* * *

Lissa gave thanks that the road crew had filled in most of the potholes in the road. She steered the Model A around a rock in the gravel road leading to Ozark, six Blue Vale scholars packed into the Ford with her. They giggled, intoxicated with anticipation. Lissa had socked her pink hat with the tiny brim forward, her blond hair peeking out. "Gives you a pixie look," Clementine, the clerk, had said.

"I know we'll bring home the trophy, Miss Massey," boasted Eileen Storm, long legs cramped in the back seat along with Orbert and Elroy Terfer, and Marla Edith's niece, Tippy Mae Maggler.

"We'll do our best," Lissa said as she glanced at the rearview mirror. "Better not brag before time. We'll just do our best. Everyone's worked hard. You must remember Spring Valley School and Dodder School have fine students too. We're facing some real challenges."

She thought of her brother Slade in Marla Maggler's play, *Breakfast at the Doons*, a riotous comedy, and how Slade believed Lissa's play, *Who Gets the Car Tonight?*, was much better. In spite of her students' huffing themselves in preparing for the contests, Lissa could feel the underneath rumble of apprehension and the threat of losing.

Lissa caught a glimpse of the dusty Wincet Chevrolet rattling along behind her, loaded with the remaining students. She wondered, too, if Marla Edith Maggler had already passed this way to get ahead of her. And was it true? Brandon Fall singing in Marla Edith's community chorus?

She chuckled when Aunt Gustie heard about it. "Jest let me climb up on that stage in Marla Maggler's chorus in my dust cap, Lissa. Way I bray, it'd sure rupture high-up Marla Maggler's community chorus. Why, I'd croak some notes Miss Marla's never, ever, heard before. Har, har, har."

"Well, Aunt Gustie, you did win the hog-calling contest back in 1910, didn't you?"

"Why, yes, child, yes. Hogs busted down the gate in the pavilion gettin to me. Nineteen-ought-eight, Lissa. Nineteen-ought-eight."

* * *

Lissa corralled her fourteen scholars into the seventh row from the front. Voices buzzed as students, teachers, men, and women filed into the auditorium in Ozark built by President Roosevelt's WPA. They hunched forward, waiting for the opening remarks and instructions.

"Miss Lissa, she's up there on the second row, Aunt Marla Edith, and look how she's dressed, gold necklace and gold earrings, bright red lipstick," Tippy Mae whispered to Lissa.

Sure enough. Lissa glanced up at Marla Edith, bobbing up and down, her face shifting back and forth between scowls at her eighth-grade boys and smiles at Waldon Hammers, who taught at Spring Valley. Lissa noticed that Marla Edith's black voile suit stretched across her hips.

Lissa, sitting next to Eileen Storm, who had the lead in their play, reached across and clasped Eileen's hand, giving her a reassuring smile.

Next Miss Halimeda Crimfield, a stocky, middle-aged English teacher, dressed in a mauve dress sporting heavy swirls and folds, stepped to the microphone.

"It's a pleasure to welcome our twenty-two country schools to the

1934 County Activity Day here in Ozark."

She cleared her throat as she read the names of the judges in the morning events and announced a variety of musical contests, monologues and readings, spelling, mathematics competition, and the one-act plays.

Butterflies fluttered in Lissa's stomach. She knew her well-prepared students must be feeling them too. Hollis Stumpff's big smile on his ruddy face heartened her.

Up ahead, Marla Edith thumped the head of lanky Buford Pitts, who sat next to Slade. Regardless of what happened today, she hoped Slade did his best for his school.

Lissa hadn't realized she would be under such stress. She whisked Elroy Terfer into Room Eight for the math contest. Then she hurried Needa Hodge to the study hall for the harmonica contest and rushed Orbert Terfer to Room Seventeen for monologues. She felt torn in a hundred directions. *Lord, give all of us strength to do our very best.*

On her way back to the auditorium when it was almost time for the quartets to climb onto the stage, Marla Edith Maggler shoved herself between a cluster of teachers, nearly stepping on Lissa's foot. "Well, Lissa Massey. Slade's been telling me that you were *worried* about your play." Marla Edith lowered her eyes, a smirk on her lips.

She wants to derail me. Don't move a face muscle. But Lissa felt her left cheek twitch. "Why, Marla Edith, I wish you and your scholars the best. Slade said that you have such a good community chorus—"

Before she could finish, Marla Edith bolted six feet past her trying to catch up with the Spring Valley teacher, Waldon Hammers, in the brown suit.

Lissa had to admit her quartet, with the Terfer twins, Louis Wincet, and Tippy Mae, failed to match Marla Edith's, especially with Georgianne Piper and Juanita Starr in it. Those youngsters were born singing. Somehow in her quartet, Tippy Mae got off-pitch as they sang "Silver Moon," and kept going flat, wilting like a milkweed plant on a hot day.

"Red ribbon. Oh, well we'll make it up. Plenty of time," she encouraged her students as she added up the scores so far. Blue on the harmonica solo, *Old Black Joe*, a white ribbon in the math contest. Elroy Terfer had broken the lead in his pencil and struggled with his fraction problem, trying to find the lowest common denominator.

Let's see, thirty-three points so far. What about Marla Edith? Lisa attempted to approximate their scores. As far as she could compute, she figured Dodder School had about thirty points. Keep it up. One-act plays and the community choruses coming up next.

Waldon Hammer's community chorus clustered near the front of the stage, lean and lanky women decked in outdated l920's dresses, announced hard times. They hummed their pitches and let loose with Will Solver up front directing as they sang, *O What a Morning*.

Poor harmony and timing. Lisa noticed Marla Edith shoot a relieved look her way.

Marla Edith's chorus marched on stage, faces wreathed in smug smiles, except for Brandon Fall. He stood with the other twenty-two, lean as Lincoln, more haggard than ever. He peeked between Tillie Shop's and Claude Dollar's shoulders to catch a glimpse of the words to *It's Only a Paper Moon*.

Lissa could see Brandon lift his head and focus his eyes on her for a moment. Was he thinking that he had been right, not pushing it, believing he had nothing to offer? If the church doesn't select him, will he go ahead and fill out an application for the Civilian Conservation Corps? Brandon's sad eyes lowered as he cleared his throat to sing.

It was evident that Marla Edith took great pleasure standing in front, skirt hiking in back due to overzealous arm and swinging hand as she directed her choir.

Strange, isn't it? Lissa thought, I don't feel a thing, staring at Brandon's face. Maybe it's that new psychology coming in. Repression? Her thoughts tangled. A poke from Eileen Storm, sitting by her, jarred Lissa from her thoughts.

Next, Blue Vale Community Chorus filed on stage while Lena Adams seated herself at the piano. Twenty-nine in all, mostly dressed in their second best, which was one step up from cotton house dresses and overalls. Nevertheless, they harmonized perfectly as Lena struck their pitches and played the short overture to *Now, on*

Land and Sea Descending.
Lissa knew her directing sank below Marla Edith's standards. Nevertheless, she knew her skirt didn't climb up in back, and her arm movements were much more graceful. Lissa had to wipe perspiration from her forehead with her handkerchief when they had finished. She followed her singers down the steps and back to their row. Just four more choruses, then the judges' reports.

* * *

"We are pleased to announce Dodder School's community chorus in first place," Miss Crimfield announced, the draped cloth around her hips sagging on the left.

Four or five of Marla Edith's scholars stood, clapped and whistled, though she tried to shove them down into their seats, ecstatic look on her olive face. Marla Edith put on her best hip walk as she bounced up to receive the ribbon, glancing back in triumph at Lissa.

Lissa thought her chorus performed better than Spring Valley's, but she had to be content again with one of those pale white ribbons. Third place.

"We was better than them." Eileen Storm struggled to rise, fury on her face. Lissa reached across to pat her thigh to calm her. She'd correct the agitated girl's English later. Lissa noticed Eileen's flushed face. Is she feverish?

She penciled in her seven points for the chorus. Now Marla Edith was ahead. Lissa's heartbeat quickened.

* * *

Lissa had to admire Slade's acting ability in Marla Edith's play, *Breakfast at the Doons.* She sat straight to catch the words flying like confetti. The student actors knew their parts, and the dialogue ricocheted back and forth.

Too raucous and overdone. Marla Edith should have selected something less slapstick. Lissa felt sorry for Slade, doing his best in an obviously tacky play. But as well as they were performing,

Dodder School just might receive first place.

"And now we will be honored with the play by Blue Vale School, *Who Gets the Car Tonight?*"

Eileen Storm, Hollis Stumpff, Lottie Wincet, and Orbert Terfer huddled behind the curtains while Lissa and Elroy shoved the couch into place. Tippy Mae Maggler bounced out with the telephone for the stand table.

They know their parts, the lines are captivating, and the drama exciting, Lissa reassured herself as she straightened the collar on her pink blouse, which had tangled under her white beads.

"Hurry, Hollis and Eileen, it's almost time to draw the curtains," Orbert rasped. Murmurings from the audience on the other side of the curtain drifted toward them. Lissa turned to face Eileen Storm, hair rolled up in back to play the middle-aged mother part, glasses across her nose, long print dress, and low-heeled shoes. "What's wrong, Eileen?"

Eileen wilted and staggered towards the side curtain. She bent over as she slouched to a ladder-back chair, face pale as dog tooth violets.

"Oh, Miss Massey, I'm sorry, but I'm sick. I'm going to vom–"

But Eileen never got to finish the word as she covered her mouth with her handkerchief. Lissa rushed to her side. She dragged the sick girl down the short flight to the stage door, flinging it open as poor Eileen heaved and gagged.

Fortunately, Lena Adams, who had played the piano for her chorus, heard the disturbance and rushed out the side door to offer help.

"Oh, Miss Massey, I can't go on stage." Poor Eileen heaved again.

Just what I deserve, caught up in this competition with Marla Edith. I deserve this punishment. Now what? Give up the play? Who could stand in for Eileen? Lissa's chin fell and her brow creased as she turned to see who was pecking her so hard on the shoulder.

"Miss Massey, Miss Massey, let me go on stage in the play. I know them lines."

There stood Tippy Mae, who diddled and dallied in her studies, failing in mathematics. Go on stage? Tippy Mae?

"Why," Lissa said, realizing that time was slipping away and the audience was growing restless. "Tippy Mae, you haven't memorized those lines, how could you? We'll just have to give it up."

"No! We're gonna beat old Aunt Marla Edith. Please, Miss Massey, I can save the play. Sittin' there in my seat watching them practice, I picked up the lines. Yes, I did." Tippy Mae shoved her broad head into Lissa's face, hot breath carrying her words. Lissa caught the drift of the fried mush and sausage Tippy Mae had for breakfast. "If you don't let me do it, I ain't gonna come to your wedding with that Reverend whatever-his-name is."

By now, Lena Adams had ushered poor Eileen back inside and down the long aisle toward the girls' rest room.

"Let Tippy Mae do it, Miss Massey," Hollis Stumpff urged, who played the father opposite Eileen. "She does know the part, Miss Massey. She said the words and went through all the motions as we walked home from school."

She couldn't believe it. What next? Her amateur actors ushered their frazzled teacher back behind the curtain. Tippy Mae wadded up her thick braid, stuck in some hairpins and grabbed the bent glasses. Her ballooning and faded skirt, ankle socks and runover shoes would have to do.

"Pull them curtains, Louis Wincet," Tippy Mae ordered. The four determined actors positioned themselves on stage. The audience hushed.

Lissa, ready to pass out, realized her scholars had taken over. Tippy Mae cavorting up there on stage, no practice? Where was the play book? She would have to prompt her.

Then Lissa realized that she'd left the play book on the seat of the Model A. Dear Lord, help them, they'll all have to wing it.

She sank into the folding chair behind the side curtain awaiting the humiliation. Blue Vale School would be the laughing stock of the county. The superintendent of schools would call her in over this. Lissa struggled to draw up her mouth, sagging due to the heavy rocks piling in her stomach.

CHAPTER ELEVEN

Lissa steered the packed Model A down the last swale before the climb to Blue Vale School. Tippy Mae's chapped hands clasped the golden trophy, an angel-like figure about to leap off a square of walnut wood. "We done it, we done it. I said we was gonna whup Marla Edith's b–"

"Tiphanie Mae Maggler!" Lissa didn't want to scold the triumphant girl and ruin her day, but Tippy Mae had crossed the line. It'd take a whole week to get her English back to something resembling respectable.

Yes, it had been a triumph. Lissa's face glowed with satisfaction. She couldn't help her broad smile. A chuckle rippled up her throat as she reviewed the day's events. Hollis Stumpff, performing the role as "father" in the play; his "son," Louis, hounding him for the family car. Tippy Mae, the last-minute "mother" defended her "daughter," Needa, who needed the car to go to the social. The drama climaxing when the four family members yelled and squabbled.

The audience howled when Tippy Mae, legs wide apart, unshakable as Molly Brown, tangled in the verbal onslaught with Hollis. Terrific, terrific. Who would have thought it?

Strands of Lissa's golden hair had fallen from beneath her hat, which had been smashed when Elroy Terfer sat on it by mistake. Her shoes reeked of vomit. My first year of teaching, and we haul off the trophy. She pushed the horn button, the "uh-ooooga, uh-ooooga"

A BRANSON LOVE

echoing in the valley below Mount Branson Bluff. They rolled in laughter and gladness in spite of the Limburger-cheese smell filling their nostrils from Elroy Terfer's ragged sneakers.

"And Miss Massey," Hollis Stumpff shouted, "we'd of lost the trophy for sure if it hadn't been for Ida Jane."

Yes, Lord, bless little Ida Jane, who had dared to call out, "Hey, twist-up Oliver Tractor," which caused Oliver Rutley to stop in his tracks. Lissa admitted that she was more than thankful for the first-grader who'd rescued them during the boy's fifty-yard dash.

With the blue ribbon from the play, they'd soared ahead of Marla Edith's troupe. Dodder school's decline had begun with the afternoon athletic events.

Since long-legged Eileen Storm's Aunt Philla had to drive her home, they'd had no one to enter the girl's one-hundred-yard dash they'd counted on winning.

Then Orbert Terfer's foot slipped when he leaned in for the broad jump, and with the faulty start, he only placed third.

"We got about seventy-six points, ain't we, Miss Massey?" Tippy Mae yelled. But Lissa had worried, according to her tally, Marla Edith had accumulated at least seventy-eight. Confronted with the boys' fifty-yard dash and Marla Edith's Oliver Rutley, heavy as a rhinoceros, leaning in for the start, they'd wrung their hands and their faces fell. Everyone knew – get surly Oliver started and he'd fly down the track like the White River Limited on the Missouri Pacific tracks.

Oliver leered back at Lissa's bedraggled crew waiting at the sideline, urging their own Louis Wincet to find a way to lunge ahead. They jumped and prayed as the coach called, "On your marks, get set...."

Coach Hyatt fired his pistol, and off lurched the eleven desperate runners.

Then little poker-faced Ida Jane, who dragged along to school with Oliver Rutley and his two quarreling sisters, knew that Oliver hated being teased, especially when the boys yelled, "Hey, twist-up Oliver tractor...."

Whenever Oliver heard those words he'd stop abruptly in his tracks, turn, scowl, and hurl threats at his tormentors.

That was when little Ida Jane pushed between Needa Hodge and Miss Massey, cupping her hands at her mouth to yell, "Hey, twist-up Oliver tractor."

Lumbering Oliver, hearing what he considered an ugly slur, stopped like a rhino who had hit a sycamore stump. The runners sped on, their own Orbert Terfer in the lead.

Red-faced Oliver glared at little Ida Jane, he puffed, rasped, and blew, "You little nerd–"

Blue Vale now soared two points ahead of Dodder School.

"Did you see Aunt Marla Edith's face?" Tippy Mae blared. "It turned green. Green, I tell you, she put her hands on her hips and blew like our heifer when she had the diarr–"

"Tiphanie Mae Maggler!" This time Lissa's voice had an edge to it. But they'd won the trophy, hadn't they?

Lissa parked by the schoolhouse steps, and the boisterous children dispersed, waving and yelling their good-byes.

Lissa, foot reeking of dried vomit, her skirt twisted, and blond strands fallen into her eyes, marched down the oiled aisle of the schoolhouse to place the shining trophy on top of the pump organ by the blackboard.

She lingered in the schoolroom, savoring the smell of the chalk, the oiled floor, and the left-over traces of sulphur belches from the coal furnace in the back. We beat Marla Edith. We won. But why do I suddenly feel so empty inside?

The evening sunlight glanced off a shiny car rolling up the side drive. What an opulent car. Who was that? Lissa stared at the dark green 1934 Oldsmobile with with white sidewalls, rocking to a halt.

Out stepped a dandy in a black suit, homburg tilting on his graying hair. A Clark Gable smile spread across his lean, swarthy face.

"Wardley, Wardley." Lissa raced to the open schoolroom door.

CHAPTER TWELVE

Next day, Lissa stepped out of the gleaming new Oldsmobile as Wardley, struggling to restrain his pride about his spanking-new new car, reached out for her gloved hand.
"We'll just walk through the house, Lissa. Maybe you'd want to think about selling Myrna's furniture and buying–"
"Wardley, no. Let's wait. With times like these? Besides, our wedding isn't until late July."
Only yesterday her mother had sliced a good portion of smoked ham to make sandwiches with her fresh bread for five homeless wanderers who'd knocked at their door, gaunt faces, eyes pleading for food. What was Brandon's point from Ephesians? "Let your moderation be made known."
The story-and-a-half brick house rose from the wide yard graced by oaks and ash. Lissa caught a glimpse of the massive weeping willow at the side. Tall spirea bushes lined the driveway. "How beautiful they'll be in the spring, Wardley."
Lissa strolled through the living room door Wardley held open for her. She caught the fragrance of bay rum drifting from his cheeks and neck. "I love the etched window in the door. Fleur-de-lis, isn't it?"
"Yes, Lissa, my dear, fleur-de-lis. We purchased that window at Pickett's up in Springfield."
Wardley closed the door and stepped nimbly over to raise the green shade behind the ecru lace curtains at the bay window which

faced the willows along the creek.

"It's beautiful, Wardley. Beautiful."

Lissa's eyes swept over the cane-and-brown velour couch and matching chair, the walnut end tables, cocktail table, the swivel rocker, then down across the wool rug with the roses. Graceful, but not extravagant. With Wardley's love, yes, it could be a lovely home.

"Electric lights. You can't believe, Wardley, how much I'll appreciate pushing a button and suddenly there is light. It's a miracle to me." Lissa wandered into the hall with the mirror and bookcase. Wardley allowed her to step away as if he realized Lissa needed time to savor the house alone.

Lissa's mind caught on her prayers last night when she had knelt by her bed so long the floor cracks left marks in her knees. "Dear Lord, forgive me for losing sight of humility and graciousness. I've gloated and sought to triumph over others today."

Marla Edith's face rose before her. "Forgive us our trespasses as we forgive.…

"Forgive me for setting a bad example for my young students. Instead of humility, I boasted. Instead of forgiveness, resentment against Marla Edith overcame me."

Then Brandon appeared before her soul's eyes.

"And dear Lord, bless Brandon, dear Brandon. He looked so forlorn and cold, Lord. Lift him up. His trials are many. May our church extend itself to him and to your calling.…"

Then it hit her. Resentment against Brandon, too?

"I hadn't realized it, Lord, but I know I've resented Brandon. Forgive me. May I find strength to comfort him with others in the church according to your grace and your love." Buried feelings of rejection, bewilderment, and even anger at Brandon's seeming indifference to her the past months surfaced.

Lissa prayed for Wardley, and for her family, but especially for Wardley and for herself.

"May I find the grace to overlook the unkind remarks people make about Wardley's and my love.… Give me the strength to be the wife Wardley needs."

She hadn't realized they'd meandered into the kitchen, where the white cupboards rose all the way to the ceiling.

"You'll appreciate this, too, Lissa." Wardley stepped across the linoleum to stand beside her and reached to turn on the water faucet at the white sink.

"Oh, yes, hot and cold water. Bathroom, too." Another miracle, her eyes caught a glimpse of the gleaming white sink and the wallpaper with the pink water lilies. She laughed, clasping his arm. Comfort flooded her spirit, and color rose in her cheeks.

When they were wandering through the modest bedrooms upstairs and the hall, Lissa noticed Wardley's shoulders slump as he stood looking out the little diamond-shaped window overlooking the street. The lines around his eyes deepened, his chin dropped as he lowered his head. This house is too much for him, bringing back the grief.

Lissa slid to his side, her fingers closed around the arm of his soft coat. She noticed how his scarf highlighted the grey in his hair. Those lines in his face.

"Wardley, perhaps we shouldn't have come today. Myrna's tragic illness, her death...."

"No, Lissa, my dear. Yes, some sorrow lingers, and it should, I suppose it's etched somewhere within me – like the fleur-de-lis. It's etched in your heart too, Lissa, from losing your dear father, Jessee."

Lissa turned fully toward him, looked up into his dark eyes as a smile returned to his lips. She threw her arms around his neck, bringing his face nearer.

"Lissa, my darling. Lissa, you make me so very happy." He kissed her waiting lips.

CHAPTER THIRTEEN

Lissa raked her hoe through the green bean plants, which looked promising after the modest spring rain. She recognized, though, that the drought wasn't over and the fragile plants could wither before they bore.

Her skin tingled at the burst of fresh wind that brushed her cheeks, dislodging a strand of hair. She realized that her feelings for Wardley Stafford were like the young, green plants, promising.

Lissa stopped, reached up to pull her sunbonnet to better shade her eyes, and turned to her Aunt Gustie, who crawled on her knees to pick potato bugs off the plant leaves, then drop them into her can of kerosene.

"I'm glad the church chose Brandon to be superintendent of the summer Bible school," Lissa said, "but I can't understand why they selected Marla Edith to lead the children's choir."

Aunt Gustie chuckled. "Child, when you reach my age, you'll stop wondering about decisions church boards make.

"It's because she's so good with children's choirs, Lissa. You know her youngsters took a blue ribbon, activity day last month. Deserved it, too." Gustie stood, hand on her back. "Course them Magglers know how to wiggle themselves up front."

Lissa realized Aunt Gustie tried to look on the positive side, especially since she was aware of Marla Edith's animosity toward Lissa, animosity heightened by her scholars' hightailing it off with the trophy the way they had done.

"Pug Beamer over at Lit Watson's store told me Marla Edith still considers getting a lawyer over the Blue Vale School deal. Then, Marla Edith said you got the trophy, Lissa, but you got it through deceit. Didn't earn it." Aunt Gustie slapped her lean thigh right where the patch had worn thin on her garden calico. Her chuckle goaded Lissa.

Lissa realized she'd been too triumphant about being rescued by impulsive Ida Jane's outcry, but she'd prayed for forgiveness for gloating, hadn't she?

If only Ella Lute's boys hadn't come down with the mumps so late in the season. Lissa thought of the fine Bible school choirs in the past under Ella's direction. That left the Sunday School superintendent hurrying to find a replacement. Marla Edith was capable, Lissa admitted to herself.

But Marla Edith was too forward, volunteering like she did, wasn't she? Practically thrusting herself on the board.

"Miss Maggler and Brandon run the whole show, don't they, Lissa?" Gustie stood, her lard can half-filled with red potato bugs.

"There was criticism among our church members about choosing Marla Edith, though Brother Supple said we'd ought to give it a try, after all. Didn't the Bible say you shouldn't quench the smoking flax?" Estra said as if she were trying to keep the smouldering flax from bursting into a prairie fire.

"Well, our church usually doesn't go outside our members for staff, especially for the children's choir. But the Bible School is for the whole community." Lissa picked up a thin stone to scrape her hoe.

"Marla Edith's been coming to White Oak services for several months now, Lissa. Magglers belonged to our church before they transferred to the town church." Estra rose from her chair, her gentle face turned toward Lissa.

Lissa knew exactly why Marla Edith had been warming benches at White Oak Church. Brandon Fall. She felt like throwing down her hoe and stalking through the woods to see if the gooseberries were going to amount to anything this season.

Brandon and Marla Edith. Brandon and Marla Edith. Chummy Marla Edith dipping her head over a neck that already bore rings of fat. Poring over the music scores with him. "Do you like this selection, Brandon? Do you think we should do it with the pump organ, or a cappella?" Couldn't he see through it?

Then the guilt overwhelmed her like a swarm of bees over a clover field. I must pray more sincerely. Why does it bother me so much? Why am I so angry about it? Her toes curled in her cracked garden shoes. Is it because I'm engaged to Wardley Stafford? And Wardley off in Little Rock with his overseeing duties. I must write him a letter this afternoon.

Lissa concluded that Brandon Fall was his own man and was perfectly capable of directing his own life. She concluded, too, that she was too picky about Marla Edith. After all, the children's singing of *Master, the Tempest is Raging* under Marla Edith's direction yesterday was amazing, wasn't it? Let bygones be bygones.

* * *

It wasn't so bad after all, teaching the sixth grade Bible School class of seven bright scholars. The studies, "Lessons by Galilee," captivated the youngsters' attention.

Brandon leaned into Lissa's curtained-off classroom just after she had dismissed the students for recess on the churchyard. Children's happy cries echoed through the open window. The wind's drift brought in the sweet smell of clover.

"Lissa, I want to tell you what a fine job you're doing. Those Psalms and passages from the Sermon on the Mount the children memorized will stay with them until adulthood." He cleared his throat as if he wondered if she was all right.

Lissa noticed his stare and wondered if he thought she'd lost weight. Maybe it's the dress I'm wearing. Brandon always said she looked best in blue.

"Thanks, Brandon, it's nice to hear the compliment. You know it's important to teach Bible stories when the children are young." She reached out to rub the fruit jar holding the field daisies, glancing away from his dark eyes.

What is it? Feels like we've both lost something and can't remember what it is. "I'll be so glad, Brandon, when the door opens for you to go to seminary. I'm glad, too, our church votes this Sunday on ordaining you. It's bound to carry. That'll help you with a small salary. The hard times'll pass, you'll see." Lissa realized her words sounded flat. Reassurance? Of what worth was reassurance?

Recess over, Brandon turned to ring the bell. Lissa's shoulders sagged from pushing herself and fatigue over teaching the children that morning. Worry, too, about helping her mother make her paltry salary stretch.

Lissa concluded she'd done the right thing. Had she gotten in Brandon's way in times like these and with his parents' pitiful situation, it would only have sidetracked him from his calling.

She recognized, too, that she was tired from rescuing people, weary from pushing herself to get her college hours, shoving herself forward for a teaching job. Weary of the dust, the dirt, the poverty, and death.

She admitted she was glad for Brandon. God bless him, and may he receive a strong vote from the church. Lissa rose to go meet her seven students at the church steps.

* * *

During the second week, Superintendent Brandon Fall collected the final Bible School offering. The children, in spite of their poverty, gladly tossed in their pennies, nickels, and dimes.

"Children, we're giving this with all our love and joy to the mission in Africa," Brandon had announced to the assembled children. Marla Edith, in a modest shirtwaist and no lipstick, smiled approvingly and tossed in a five-dollar bill.

"Lissa, would you help me count the two-weeks' offering?"

Now why had Brandon called on her to do that? Lissa nodded her head. At the side table during the break, they counted and sorted the nickles, pennies, and dimes and Marla's five-dollar bill. Lissa and Brandon agreed their count was the same, forty dollars.

"We all agree on sending this to Reverend J. Moody Maggler, Congo African Mission, right?" Brandon asked. Reverend J. Moody Maggler just happened to be Marla Edith's cousin, Lissa knew.

"I'll send it to Cousin Moody," volunteered Marla Edith as she tugged at the green glass beads against her olive neck. "Save you the trouble, Brandon. You have enough to do. Besides, I have his address in the secretary at home. Get it off in a money order this week."

Lissa, who couldn't help seeing the look on Marla Edith's face, thought, she's doing it on purpose, taking control, butting in. It really isn't her responsibility.

Then guilt pressed her heart along with buried sadness. What did happen to Brandon and me? Why haven't we seriously talked about it? I know he can't marry now with his responsibilities, but....

Lissa stepped to her mother's dust-covered Model A. She hit the starter with her heel. Wardley. Dear, dear Wardley. I must write him a letter when I get home. I know he's lonely down in Little Rock. She tried to focus her mind on his chisled face, his salt-and-pepper-hair, his curving lips....

As the Ford rattled over the road toward home, Lissa struggled with her feelings, mixed as a neglected flowerbed of larkspur and mustard weed. Shoved to one side. Anyone could have taught my sixth grade. Brandon didn't even thank me. Marla Edith letting me know in my own church that she was "higher up" than I, directing the choir and all.

Lissa realized she'd better pitch a damp towel over her heated feelings or she would be a sorry mess in front of her class at the program tonight.

She also admitted that she was piqued at her handsome Wardley Stafford staying so long in Little Rock trying to organize a new congregation there.

Yes, I'd better get home and write Wardley a letter. She recognized the stability, the strength, and power he exuded. After all, hadn't she had enough of shifting relationships?

Dust flew behind the Model A, gravel pinged against the fenders and runningboard. She slowed the Ford in order to maneuver the turn over the culvert and into the lane where the purple bee balm grew. The four front windows of the farmhouse stared at her.

CHAPTER FOURTEEN

Members of White Oak Church lifted their heads, eyes focusing toward the ancient pulpit, hearts beating, ready to soak up Reverend Stafford's sermon on Christian Duty.

All, that is, except one man seated on the second row to the left from the back. The man, with the shaggy hair around his shirt collar, dug a toothpick from his pocket, inserted it in his mouth and braced his knees against the songbook rack. The toothpick wagged from his tongue movements.

For the third time Wardley noticed Rennart's face, an air of disinterest spread across it. *That brother not agreeing with me? Have I said something offensive? Is he put off?* The thoughts interrupted the flow of his sentences.

Wardley turned to the right, warmed by the sight of Lissa in a prim navy suit and matching cloche hat, seated by Estra and Slade, Bibles opened, attuned. He regained his stride.

He'd noticed the Rennart brother before, especially when he remembered that he was a deacon and that the man's daughter, Reva, was engaged to marry that senior St. Mark seminary student in Kansas City, Elwin Nevins. But where had he seen him before?

* * *

Brandon Fall, seated beside retiring Preacher Supple behind the pulpit, noticed Rennart, toothpick wagging, eyes focusing up to the ceiling. Was the service too long? Brandon glanced up at the clock, but it was only twenty-to-twelve.

Brandon sat bathed in the comfort of the congregational vote two weeks ago to ordain him and support him in his ministry. "In time, God will open doors for you to get to either seminary or Bible school," their aged minister, Ezra Supple, had said. "You have an almost ninety percent vote, Brandon, and both I and Reverend Stafford affirm you."

At least a salary of seventy dollars a month. I can look for another car. He pondered that thought for a moment. He smiled, noticing Marla Edith seated on the third row from the back, dressed this time in modest brown. She seemed aware of his glance and smiled at him, then folded her gloved hands.

Brandon knew his mind was wandering, thinking of Marla Edith's support and her willing friendship. Seeing her stimulated his thoughts about her. Someday she'll meet the right man, someone her age. Maybe a widower. God knows. Charlie Kenton, or Alf Tracy, both widowers in this church – one would have thought they'd have interest in a fine-looking woman like Marla Edith.

Service over, Wardley Stafford and Brandon Fall stood as usual in the vestibule to greet and receive greetings from friends and neighbors.

"Interesting way of looking at our Christian duties, your sermon." Rhutley Rennart reached out a hairy paw to shake hands with Wardley, but before moving on to Brandon, he said in a lowered voice, "Like to visit with ya, Wardley, in the west Sunday School room when you finish here." He cleared his throat and pulled on the lapel of his wrinkled suit.

He wants to look deeper into the matter of the Christian life, Wardley hoped. "Why, yes, brother...."

"Rennart, one of the deacons here, but I missed those ministerial search committee meetings you led." The crowd closed around Rennart. Brandon and Wardley continued their nodding, bowing, hand shaking, and greeting.

Rennart was leaning against a bookcase, foot up on a folding chair, still chewing on his toothpick, when Wardley finally found his way to the Sunday School room.

A BRANSON LOVE

"Here I am, Rhutley. Rhutley Rennart, you say? Where have I heard that name? Seems like I've met you before. Give me time, it'll come to me."

"While you're here, brother Wardley, why don't we both sit down." Rennart dragged two of the wooden folding chairs away from a table. Wardley, throat hoarse from preaching, took out a white handkerchief to wipe perspiration from his forehead.

Silence hung between them. A huge black crow settled on a dead elm branch just outside the window. "Seems like I ought to know you," Wardley said again. Musty odors of old hymnals on a bookshelf engulfed them.

"You supported ordaining Brandon Fall, even without him having any formal training." Rennart's green-grey eyes focused on Stafford's black onyx ones.

"Well, yes, I support that. Fine young man, Brandon Fall. You've heard his sermons. Gifted. Make a fine minister with some training." Wardley realized Rennart wasn't going to criticize his sermon, after all.

"You go along with the board on the vote to select Fall, then?" Rhutley's cold eyes challenged Wardley like the eyes of a used-car salesman discrediting a pinched-faced customer's inadequate offer.

What was this? Why was he asking that now? Wardley straightened his back and stared straight at Rennart. Was there a serious problem? Then it hit him.

"Rhutley Rennart. You're Reva Rennart's father, aren't you, engaged to that seminary senior, Elwin Nevins. That's the connection." Is there something else? Thoughts coursed through his head.

"That's what I wanted to discuss with you, Reverend." Rennart hawked and cleared his throat again, toothpick wagging. Reaching into his coat pocket, he pulled out a folded letter. "Something here I want to go over with you since you have the power in placing young ministers. *Seminary-graduated* ones."

Something bubbling underneath. What is it? Wardley's thumb rubbed a forefinger.

"Well, yes. Hard times like these, depression everywhere, church openings near impossible to find. Brandon Fall's fortunate, Ezra

Supple stepping down and so many folks here supporting his appointment." That ought to clarify it.

Rennart rubbed his ruddy jaw with the palm of his hand. "Fall's not seminary-trained. You know that. Not even a Bible school class in Springfield." His small pig eyes bored in on Wardley's face.

"That a serious problem to you, Brother Rennart? He's a self-educated man, Rennart. The board approved him, and he got such a positive congregational vote. I'm afraid you're too late."

"Read Elwin's letter, the paragraph I marked." Rennart shoved the wrinkled letter to Wardley, stabbing at it with a stained finger.

...since Reva kept me informed about the need for a minister at White Oak Church, I would like to make a formal application as a candidate. As you know, I graduated cum laude at St. Mark Seminary. It's hard to believe, the depression and drought, there seem to be no openings, therefore....

I'll have to handle this carefully. Sensitive issue, Wardley concluded to himself. Wardley folded the letter and handed it back to Rennart.

"Understandable how the young man feels. Schools closing – churches cutting staff. Limited opportunities everywhere. I have hope, Rhutley, it'll change." Where did I know this man before? So many churches in my district. Wardley's head throbbed.

"I'd like the search committee and the board to consider Elwin Nevins an applicant for our opening at White Oak Church, *Reverend* Stafford." He licked his cracked lips with the tip of his tongue.

"But as you well know, the congregation has voted, Brother Rennart. Brandon got an extraordinarily high vote. I'm sorry, but your letter's just too late." Wardley shifted his position on his chair.

"Then there's business I need to clear up, Stafford. I'll be talking to the church board here, maybe to the head of our conference."

"Are you talking about *me*? If you are, say so, Rennart. I get a thinly veiled hint that something's.... Is there something I should know about Brandon Fall?"

Rennart stood and shuffled close enough to Stafford that Wardley noticed the ungroomed eyebrows and red nose hairs.

"No, not really about Brandon Fall, though there's a lot of talk about him spending time with that Maggler woman. You do know she was fired from Blue Vale School, don't you?"

"If it's not about Fall, then it must be about me. Is that it? You've a bone to pick with me?" Stafford lifted his tired shoulders. He'd dealt with difficult people like this from time to time. Mustn't yield to a cotton patch farmer like Rennart whose hidden interest was bringing his baby daughter and her fiancé back home. He would have to face reality.

"I really need to go, Brother Rennart, perhaps–"

"You don't remember when we met before, Stafford?"

Wardley took a step back, staring at the square chin, razor cut on the left side, the scimitar-like jaw bones, the ruddy, raw forehead. "Rhutley Rennart. Rhutley Rennart?"

"It was a long time ago, Stafford. Try thinking about seminary days in Memphis, twenty-five years ago."

Seminary? This moldy-looking farmer in seminary in Memphis with me? Wardley's mind searched.

Then Rennart, pocketing his letter in the suit with the gravy spots on the lapels, loped out.

The walls of the stuffy little room closed in on Wardley. He gasped for a breath of air. A spider dropped from a gossamer thread onto his shoulder. Perspiration broke out on his forehead.

Well, he concluded, he couldn't fault a man for favoring his daughter and son-in-law. He stuffed his trembling hands into his pants pockets. Then it struck him: Rennart – two of them, Enis and red-headed Rutley. One a bent-over scholar, who devoured ancient texts, the other, a hit-and-miss student who shouldn't even have been in seminary. And that *Church History test.*

CHAPTER FIFTEEN

"I love trumpet vine when it blooms, Wardley," Lissa said. "Drought or wet season, it always stretches itself to blossom. You can almost hear the little orange flowers trumpeting *A Mighty Fortress Is Our God*.

Arm in arm, Wardley and Lissa strolled down the path in the rock-walled city park that led to the vine-covered gazebo.

Wardley brushed some fallen ivy leaves from the bench. His white shirt, fresh from Tildy's Laundry, smelled sweet and clean. His black tie cascaded down his broad chest. Lissa's hand in his, they seated themselves, facing the river, which mirrored the leaning willows. A cardinal called, "Sweet cheer, sweet cheer, cheer, cheer, cheer."

"Lissa, my love. How can I keep on waiting? Let's go find your Preacher Supple this afternoon," Wardley teased. "You hear the cardinal cheering us on." He bent to brush her lips with his.

"It's only two more months, Wardley." Lissa smiled, face tilted up at his tanned face. She noted the healthy light in his dark eyes. Her fingers pressed tenderly into his arm muscle.

"This afternoon I want you to go down to Bradley's Furniture with me to select a new kitchen linoleum, Lissa."

Lissa lowered her fingers from his arm to his warm hand, leaned her head against his broad chest where she could hear his beating heart. "Wardley, you're so good to me. Maybe we should wait until–"

"Only the best for my Lissa. Wouldn't want you tracking around on an old linoleum where the pattern is so faded you might lose your way." He chuckled, drawing her closer.

Lissa thought of the times. She had already looked at the electric irons in Buzby's Hardware, noticing that the cheapest one was two dollars. No, times like these, I'll only mention small things for wedding gifts.

Lissa had noticed the bath towels were twenty-four cents each. Sewing circle ladies might be able to afford shower presents like those. She had to consider what people were going through.

Lissa thought of Slade, how hard he worked with Wallace, the hired man, helping him get the corn planted and cultivated, while everyone prayed for summer rains.

How carefully Slade had followed his mother's instructions about the radio. "Pick one program, son. You know the battery has to last a long time. If it conks out, we won't be able to afford another one."

So Slade ate his Wheaties and selected one program, *Jack Armstrong*, the all-American-boy's pure-in-heart Jack Armstrong, leading Hudson High to athletic glories.

Lissa smiled, knowing her brother's love for and dedication to his champion. Then she remembered. Ovaltine. Mother got those Shirley Temple glass pieces every time she bought another can of Ovaltine. She needed only two more to make a set of tumblers. And Quaker Oats gave a nice piece of Cabbage Rose depression glass with every purchase, didn't it? Sewing circle ladies wouldn't need to spend much with gifts like that. She would just let them know how many more she needed for a set.

Wardley insisted on treating Lissa to lunch at Blossom's Restaurant on South Main. She had to admit the corned beef and cabbage tasted plain heavenly with the rye bread, plus the dip of vanilla ice cream Wardley had insisted on for dessert – all for twenty-five cents each. Lissa wasn't sure how much a churchman like Wardley's salary was, but considering how well off he seemed, she guessed she needn't worry. Still, she vowed to keep close tabs on what she spent.

"Good-bye, my dove, we'll meet in church Sunday. How about me taking your mother and Slade along, all four of us to that

Springfield restaurant? I believe I promised you, day of a very embarrassing crossing at Dodie Creek. And oh, Aunt Gustie, too."

"Why, Mother and Slade'd be pleased. Aunt Gustie? Well, I believe she's a little stuck on you, Wardley – have to be on your guard." Lissa smiled. "Good-bye, Wardley."

Lissa slid out of the purring Olds which still smelled of lacquer and intoxicating newness, while Wardley drove off for a meeting Rhutley Rennart had scheduled that afternoon.

* * *

Rounding the curve where the wild plums leaned toward the ditch, it suddenly came to Wardley. His dream last night. Bits and pieces flying like leaves falling from an elm in dry season.

Edenvale Seminary in Memphis – a long time ago. Rhutley's face. Pimply and red, greasy hair falling down his face. Recalled that Rhutley worked in the library. What was a man like Rhutley Rennart doing in seminary, anyway?

What happened that Rhutley didn't graduate? What was it? Did he drop out, or fail? Well, maybe he would find out this afternoon. Whatever it was, the man certainly was building up a contentious steam. Thoughts buzzed in his mind.

As he drove, Wardley whispered to himself. "Yes. Rennart and I were in Church History. THAT Church History class? It couldn't be. Not after all these years. That final test. Wardley belched as sour bile gurgled up his throat. Under Doctor Bechert. How could I forget Rennart's groaning at test time, especially the long final?" He thought of Rennart's wrinkled pants and greasy shirt collars. Wardley recalled his own triumph, ending the semester by being the valedictorian of the class. Suddenly, Wardley was aware that his underarm deodorant had broken down and that his shirt collar was drenched with sweat.

"Maybe that's it," Wardley mumbled. "I succeeded and he didn't. He's jealous and angry and plans to interrupt what the church already decided about Brandon Fall's being selected. Embarrass me, cause me problems. Well, we'll see." Wardley swallowed another gurgle of sour bile in his throat as he tightened his resolve.

* * *

Rennart's old Chevrolet leaned under a scraggly burr oak, passenger-side door open, pigeon dirt streaking the side. Shirt sweat-stained, he lounged back in the car seat. Raking his hand through his red bristly hair, he smiled across at the successful churchman steering a new Oldsmobile in beside him.

"Come on over." Rennart waved his red-bristled paw, obviously unwilling to put himself out for Wardley Stafford.

"Hello, Rhutley. Be right over." Wardley realized it would be better if they went inside the church, sit in a classroom. More private, more seemly, but....

Wardley left his coat folded over the Olds' seat, unbuttoned his shirt collar, loosened his tie, while stepping behind his car and into the motley-colored Chevrolet with dried mud coating the running board and fenders. Wardley slid in on the dirty seat, rank odors of tobacco smoke and grease filled his nostrils. He kicked a Valvoline oil can aside with his shoe and slammed the tinny door.

"Rhutley, I remembered where I met you before. You were a library assistant and part-time student at Edenvale seminary with me. Sat beside me in Doctor Bechert's church history class." Wardley decided not to mention Rhutley's reeking feet in those tennis shoes. Forget and forgive.

"I thought it'd come to you. Yep. Seminary. Imagine me in seminary?" He snickered and wiped saliva on his lip. "My brother Enis an me both there in nineteen eleven. Good year, 'cept the snow come all the way down to Memphis, an me with no long underwear." Rhutley snickered again, as he turned glassy eyes upon Wardley.

"Well, it indeed was a cold winter as I remember it, too. But what does this have to do with me or with Brandon Fall being selected for the church?" He stared at Rennart, wondering how it was that a down-at-the-heels-looking man like Rennart had such a fine daughter, Reva. She must take after her mother's side of the family.
THAT FINAL TEST.

"What I'm asking this afternoon, Stafford, is for you to march up in front of the White Oak Church, come Sunday. Announce to the congregation that you ain't gonna support Fall after all, being's he's got no seminary training and we got us a *cu-me laud-ee,* however you say it, candidate, Elwin Nevins." Rhutley hacked and spat out his open window.

"Really, Brother Rhutley, I'm not able to do that, and I did make it clear to you before where I stood." Wardley fidgeted in his pocket for his silver-plated penknife.

"Well then, I guess I have to go to the church board, and maybe even to the conference head, Bishop Howard." Rhutley's eyes bulged like the eyes of a chilled frog.

"That's a direct threat, Rhutley. What is it? I'm asking you to lay it out for me. Whatever it is, it can be worked through." Had Brandon compromised himself?

Wardley's face tightened. His shirt collar felt wet. His curved lips slid into a rigid line. He focused his dark eyes as he realized they must be shiny as Anthracite coal.

"You're a fake, Stafford." Rhutley snickered, spat out the open window, then wiped his red-peppered chin with the butt of his palm. "Passing yourself off as a high-up leader in the church when you ain't nothing but a cheat."

Lord, have mercy. What was he referring to? How had he climbed into a car with a deranged man? How his speech had vulgarized through the years. Wardley's shoulder twitched.

"You're going to have to be clearer than that, Rhutley. I'm aware now that you have something against me personally and that it possibly goes back to our seminary days. Am I right?" Wardley's throat burned. His heart started to pound faster.

"You're beginning to get it." Rhutley spat again. He reached into his hip pocket, pulled out a soured red handkerchief and wiped spittle from his lips.

Wardley's crisp starched shirt wilted in his body heat. He could feel the warning of a creeping anger. He realized he must watch himself in order not to deepen the problem.

"My brother, Enis, was the salut-a-torian." Rhutley coughed, "However you say that word."

"What does that have to do with me?" Then it hit Wardley. Rhutley's brother, Enis, the stoop-shouldered, forever-in-the-library-and-archives one, was indeed second in their graduating class.

"Well, I was valedictorian, yes, Rhutley. But what's the point?" Should he go ahead and step right out of the car?

"Your furrow didn't go all the way to the end of the cornfield, Wardley."

"What? What did you say?" Wardley had a fleeting vision of pouring over Greek and Hebrew texts. The voluminous concordances and dictionaries, the....

"You cheated, Wardley Stafford, and I can prove it. You never earned them points. Enis always said there were only three points between him and you. Without you cheating on the final in Church History, Enis would of been valedictorian." Rhutley hacked and spat again.

Now Wardley Stafford felt a chilling coldness creep through him. Thoughts ricocheted like a stray ping-pong ball in his head. I'll have to tell him he's delusional. How far is it to the asylum over at Nevada? How did Rhutley get from seminary to this backwoods farm? How far had he fallen? Or was it Wardley who had fallen?

"I can't imagine what you're referring to, Rhutley Rennart. Let's hear the proof, whatever it is. I didn't plow all the way to the end of the field?"

Rhutley seemed more agitated, and anger streaked his face. Still, he proceeded as if assured he was a master at handling controversy. "Yep. Betcha you would want to know. Well, you forget that I was a fair scholar in them days. Good thing I sat by you in Bechert's church history. You wouldn't happen to remember the question, counted fifty points, question about 'Have you read Dollinger's *The Re-union of the Churches*'?"

"That was so long ago. But yes, I do faintly remember."

"Well, I have proof you lied on the test. Cheated."

Wardley's chest tightened at the hot, close air in the car, nausea crept through his stomach. "I-I can't possibly remember what you're referring to, Rhutley. I'm sure there's an explanation." Wardley's foot hit the Valvoline can.

"I got the explanation, Stafford. I worked in the library, and I took Bechert's Church History class. Brain-buster of a class. I only made a D-minus. Never put myself up as an egghead like you and Enis done. Course, all things eventually even out." He grinned, showing stained teeth and the tip of his tongue. "Besides, I dropped out next year anyway to marry Bertie Spindle."

"Well, yes, but what does Dollinger's book on *The Re-union of the Churches* have to do with it?"

"You never read the book, Stafford. Only one copy on reserve in the Spikert Library. Old Prof Bechert had us over a barrel. Counted fifty points, that question. Four liars in the class checked 'yes' on the test.

"Well, I hurried over to the library to my work station, and Wardley Stafford, your name never showed up on the check-out card. You was one of them cheats." Rhutley snickered.

Now the anger subsided, but Wardley's heart pounded even more. His hand trembled as he fumbled for the door handle. So long ago, now he remembered. I remember the question. I checked "yes." I thought I'd hurry over to the library and read the book right after class, but it had been withdrawn from the reserve shelf. We were caught. Old Prof Bechert must have known. And this weevil, Rhutley. I tried to forget it…. Oh, God above, forgive.…

Wardley staggered out of the Chevrolet as Rhutley ground the starter, his face grinning victory. The car backfired, underscoring Rhutley's triumph.

"The conference, nor White Oak Church board, want to hear about how our *im-portant* churchman compromised hisself back then, do you think, Stafford? Way I look at it, you didn't earn your high class rank, and you're living a lie. What else didn't you earn?"

The car wheels spun gravel, and the old Chevrolet teetered and rocked down the road.

Wardley turned toward his Olds, now dust-covered. He gripped his touseled head with both hands to steady the sudden palsy. "Dear God, what's going to unravel?" he groaned.

CHAPTER SIXTEEN

Wardley Stafford's sweaty body twisted and tangled in the sheets as he tossed in his bed. "Oh, Lord, oh, Lord...." he called out at the ceiling, belly encased in his hands.

About to wed the loveliest girl in the state, thinking about an early retirement, now faced with Peter-Tumbledown Rennart. That country hick was going to blast everything to perdition. Wardley's thoughts boiled like steam in a pressure cooker.

Then the guilt twisted his guts. A tinge of a whine edged his voice. "I've tiptoed through back-slapping and rebukes. Wouldn't be where I am today if I hadn't. Lord, Lord, don't hold such a small matter against me." His tongue trembled.

Wardley found he couldn't pray, either. Only short exclamations and gutteral pleadings to the Lord.

Then cold emptiness and agony.

"I'll have to do something. Can't let an innocent young man lose his opportunity by the crazy wiles of a rube like Rennart, can I?" He didn't realize he was talking out loud. But, he thought, why am I downing Rennart?

"Oh, Lord, Lord, Lord," he wailed. He slid out of the tumbled bed. He picked his way down the narrow staircase to circle the rooms in his bare feet, craggy head in his hands. Where's the moon? Why is it so dark?

For want of a nail, the shoe was lost ... for want of a shoe, the horse.... His feverish mind whirled. His head ached as if his brain was begining to swell. Gut-wrenching guilt gushed up from below.

"Lissa, Lissa, my angel Lissa. Oh, Lord, I'll lose Lissa over this if I don't...." Words failed.

Wardley Stafford even called out to his wife, Myrna, under the little mound in Rose Cemetery. "Myrna, Myrna, plead for me. Yes, maybe a little mistake, but you found me to be a good man, didn't you? Well, a little pompous at times. Who could hold that book incident against a student, young, scraping to make it? God knows how hard I tried."

Myrna's bones gave no consolation. No mercy descended from heaven above. Only silence. Then the wind picked up. Was that thunder? A howling rush tore at the eaves of the house.

Wardley thought of his bank account. Shouldn't have bought that new car. Money. Would the bumbling hog farmer take money? How much? Why, my account is down.... Oh, Lord!

* * *

Aunt Gustie decided she was well enough to go to services, being as her favorite neighbor, Brandon Fall, was going to be put forth for ordination for the ministry. How did it happen that he and Lissa didn't...?

The Ford hit the bump at the lane culvert. Gustie's hat, purchased at Tillie's back in 1919, slid to the side. Estra, in front with Lissa, reached up with one hand to steady her black straw with the flattened burgundy rose at the black bow. "My, Lissa, we've got time. Know the church'll be crowded, but better slow down."

A glowing feeling flowed through Lissa's veins and all the way down to her foot on the gas pedal. Cheerfulness, joy, faith in what the future held, and yes, even a great warmth for her gallant man, Wardley Stafford, surged in her heart. He'd be dressed so handsomely in his best black, unaware of how charming the ladies thought he was when he absent-mindedly raked his left hand through his hair as he stood behind the pulpit. And his voice, Wardley's voice – deep, cultured enunciations, soul-soothing.

A perfect, blissful day. Brandon getting the boost he needed. Her thoughts lightened her heart. Thank you, Lord, for answering prayer.

Lissa turned the Model A, which Slade had washed only yesterday at the edge of the pond, into the fast-filling churchyard.

"My, Birdie and Rhutley Rennart are here early today," Lissa said as she stepped out and joined Slade. Lissa noticed Birdie in her off-color orange dress and faded yellow hat, and Rhutley's suit, which looked like one of their rust-colored hounds had slept on it. But she saw the determination in their step. Lissa wondered how the Rennarts raised a petite and mannerly daughter like Reva, anyway. Landing that scholarly seminarian, Elwin Nevins.

The parishoners greeted each other and lowered their voices as they approached the worship hour. Lissa's ears picked up what seemed to be the sounds of a crutch on the hard oak boards. She turned to glance. Brandon's frail father, Owney, limp arm swinging, good arm and hand clutching a crutch, struggled down the aisle. A thin tie hung from his clean but threadbare striped shirt that Serena had ironed for him with her sad iron.

And Serena's face, wrinkled and pale, but beaming. Her starched cotton dress fresh and clean. Poor woman, her back twisted and bowed.

Lissa was glad that Owney and Serena found the strength to venture out on this day. Serena helped the struggling man to the front bench and the space reserved for them. They waited patiently for the distinguished Stafford to announce the details of Brandon's ordination.

The old couple lifted faces reflecting their prayerful attention and concern for Brandon. Soon they all expected Brandon to step out of the little side office and take one of the three chairs behind the pulpit.

"Did you notice, Lissa, Rhutley Rennart must be going to have a part in the service. He got up and walked over to the pastor's office," Estra whispered.

Lissa knew that Wardley would probably involve at least one of the deacons. Why Rhutley? She noticed dear retired Ezra Supple on the left front bench, smiling as if he was breathing a prayer of thanks to God for raising up such a stalwart servant as Brandon among them.

The song leader raised a hymnal in his big farmer's hand and led the congregation in *How Firm a Foundation*. Ida Lou Swank, rocking and pumping lustily, provided backdrop on the little organ.

Scripture, sure enough, read by Rhutley Rennart, wrinkled suit, or no wrinkled suit. From Psalm fifty? How strange. "When thou sawest a thief, thou contendest with him, and hast been partaker with adulterers.... These things hast thou done, and I kept silence...."

Rhutley coughed as if clearing phlegm from his throat, searched over the congregation with cold blue eyes, then turned as if to see if black-clothed Stafford was still anchored in the oak chair behind him.

Then it hit Lissa. Where is Brandon? Why isn't he seated behind the pulpit with Wardley?

Then Lissa noticed Wardley's fallen face as she leaned forward to get a better look around Elizabeth Spivel's broad-brimmed hat.

Why, I believe Wardley's sick, slouching there behind the pulpit. That's why Rhutley's reading the Scripture. Lissa turned to her mother, who was following the verses in her open Bible.

When Wardley Stafford, overseer of the congregations of Missouri and Arkansas, rose to greet them, it was obvious. Their stalwart and dear leader was definitely ill.

Those haggard lines on each side of his face. Does he have the flu? His hair. Did he brush it at all this morning? I never saw Wardley with his shirt collar turning up and his tie askew. What is the matter...?

Pity for him jabbed her heart. Why hadn't he let her know? What on earth was causing him such pain?

"Brothers and sisters of White Oak Church." Wardley's voice sounded like a stick scraping over a corrugated corn crib roof.

The broad-shouldered, powerful man sagged, coattails hanging on each side of the pulpit. His big hand trembled as he raked it through his poorly groomed hair and back again.

What is it? Look at his eyes. Tears crept to the corners of Lissa's eyes. By now Estra's twistings told Lissa that she, too, was aware that something was off course, way, way off course.

Wardley turned a pain-mapped face to the left and to the right. He cleared his throat; a wobbling hand attempted to steady lips which kept wanting to tremble and turn downward.

"Brothers and sisters, we, uh – I must make an announcement. You must listen carefully. The announcement comes with the authority vested in the conference and with the approval of its Conference Minister, namely, me, Wardley Stafford."

Church members shifted their positions for a better glimpse of the powerful clergyman before them, lips twisting, his body twitching.

"I'm announcing today that the decision this congregation made in its approval of Brother Brandon Fall as a candidate for ordination and assignment to this pulpit will not go forward."

Gasping spread through the congregaton. A loud thump echoed in front where Brandon's father, Owney, lost grip on his crutch and it hit the floor. Serena, already leaning forward on account of her bowed back, rocked back and forth as if stricken by a stroke, her trembling hand searching for her mouth.

"Why? Wardley, why? What's going on?" Lissa mouthed the words, and tears streamed down her cheeks. Slade leaned toward her, his face fallen in dismay.

"As your overseer appointed by the conference, my authority prevails. The decision to ordain Brother Fall is hereby rescinded. God has led...." Wardley's voice failed. He twisted his shoulders.

"The deacons here in your church, led, may I say, by Brother Rhutley Rennart, announce a *new* candidate for your pulpit, a fine seminary graduate whom I'm sure you all know or know about, Brother Elwin Nevins."

Wardley covered his mouth to cough and clear his throat as if it were desert dry, trying to mouth those terrible words, "When I kept silence, my bones waxed old through my roaring all day long...."

Lissa didn't remember much more of the service, but she knew Wardley should never have tried to preach after such an announcement.

I must see him. I must go to him. Wardley, Wardley, what's happening? Lissa twisted her handkerchief. Then it hit her, the shattering pain and disbelief her old friend, Brandon Fall, must be suffering. "Dear Lord, surround him with all your holy and comforting angels," she whispered.

CHAPTER SEVENTEEN

Following Wardley's stumble-worded benediction, Lissa pushed through the aisle, where folks stood, on hearing the good news, to pat the backs and shake hands with the Rennarts, while others staggered outside with drawn faces, shaking their heads.

Lissa grabbed Wardley's coat sleeve and dragged him to the side office, not realizing how hard she'd slammed the door.

"Wardley. Wardley. What is it? Why didn't you tell me?" Tears streamed down both cheeks. "Oh, Wardley, poor Serena and Owney. Did you see them staggering and weeping?"

Wardley sagged in the desk chair, forcing himself to turn his haggard face toward Lissa. "I-I, Lissa, I couldn't bring myself to...."

"Why? What is it? Has Brandon disqualified himself somehow? Is it Marla Edith?" Lissa drew a wooden folding chair beside him and reached for his hand.

"In time, Lissa. In time, maybe I'll be able to go over it so you will understand." He sagged lower in the chair, buried his face in his hands as if he considered himself cowardly.

"If you can't tell me now, Wardley, then I'm going to go home with my family. Whatever it is, you must tell me. I simply cannot live with this and not know." Lissa looked straight into his despairing eyes.

Someone rapped at the office door Lissa had slammed so tightly. Leaning over, she opened it part way. There stood Marla Edith Maggler in her crisp navy suit and matching gloves and hat. Marla

A BRANSON LOVE

Edith dipped her head in what was obviously meant to be respect. "Why, pardon me, Lissa Massey. I took notice, well, as everybody did, that Reverend Stafford may be ill. Is there anything I can do?" Again, her head lowered in deference.

"Why, why – thank you, Marla Edith. No, Reverend Stafford just needs some time to be alone. He's feeling better, and surely some rest will help him." Lissa closed the door. Wasn't that a surprise?

"Who was it, Lissa, something I need to attend to?"

"No, Wardley. It was Marla Edith Maggler inquiring if she could help. She believed you were ill."

Wardley raised his head and his glassy eyes searched beyond the small window to where the country folk were loading up, starting their cars and driving off in clouds of dust.

"Let me come over tonight, Lissa. Give me a little time." Explain? Yes. Explain. He groaned. "There are some things I have to work through." He stood, but Lissa noticed his hands were trembling, his face ashen.

"Yes, go with your mother and brother now. I'll honor you all with that dinner in Springfield some other...." His voice faded. His cold hand reached for Lissa. She let him hold her, but only for a moment. She didn't offer lips or cheek for his kiss.

As Lissa edged toward her waiting family in the Model A, the thought pushed at her brain – there's another man I must see, and I must see him today. Brandon. Brandon.

CHAPTER EIGHTEEN

Lissa couldn't fork down a single morsel at their Sunday table, where all the faces fell and the conversation ground to a halt like the cream separator every evening.

"I'll be back later," she said as she stepped out the kitchen porch door and headed for the car.

"Well, we don't need to guess where she's going, do we?" Aunt Gustie pushed her plate back, cold gravy glazing her mashed potatoes. "I always knew you couldn't trust them high-up churchmen. Looks as if our Lissa ain't gonna be able to leap over the hurdle Stafford had the gall to throw up today." Gustie hacked and dug in her apron pocket for her red farmer's handkerchief.

"We mustn't make hasty judgments, Gustie. The poor man was under a great stress. There's a reason, and the Lord has his ways. We must pray for him." Estra pushed a green tumbler back from her plate.

"But why? Why?" Slade rose. "Is it all right if I'm excused, Mother? I'm not hungry."

The afternoon stretched before the Masseys, desolate as that Death Valley place out in California Slade had learned about on the radio.

* * *

A BRANSON LOVE

Dust hadn't even settled around her Ford when Brandon leaned out of the patched screen door. "Let's walk down to the Dodie Creek footbridge, Lissa." His eyes told her that there, in their old place, secrets and heart-pains could be revealed.

They sat on the broad limb of the mulberry by the rugged bridge. "Tell me, Brandon, why you were shoved aside? What is it?" Her intense eyes searched his face. She had already decided not to bring up the question, "Why did you leave me stranded by the footbridge that evening?"

"You know, Lissa, that announcement was as much a surprise to me as it was to you and most of the others. I just don't know, except that it's true, Elwin Nevins is a fine graduate up at St. Mark Seminary, and he'll make a first-class minister."

Lissa reached out to take his hand. How warm and comforting it felt, and callused – not at all like Wardley's soft hand. It was as if Brandon extended comfort to her, seeing how shaken she was.

Brandon turned his lean face downward to look into her soulful eyes. "Lissa, I read in the *Ozark Times* that thousands of churches across the land had to let their ministers go, couldn't afford them. In times like these, it's only right that the well-trained be selected first." He removed his hand from Lissa's, eyes glancing at the trickle in Dodie Creek.

"What will you do now, Brandon?" She searched his face. Oh, why didn't I drive over to his house the night we moved those smelly pullets? A wind from Inspiration Point swept down through the valley.

"Me? Well, I'm going to the Civilian Conservation Corps office over in Ozark tomorrow, if I can get the Model T started. Maybe have to ride old Dink. Ought to have done it months ago." Brandon looked down at a lonely toad hopping toward the creek.

Lissa's eyes widened, her chin fell and her heart skipped a beat. The CCC? Away from here? Building a dam on the Colorado River, miles from here? Pain shot through her forehead. She lifted her face, her eyes scanning for answers as she thought, I'd forgotten how his thick brown hair curls. But Wardley. I'm engaged to Wardley, and today he's suffering so. Lord, Lord, I'm so confused....

Lissa wanted to ask, "Does Marla Edith have anything to do with

Wardley's decision today?" but she didn't need to. Brandon himself enlightened her.

"I suppose some folks think maybe Marla Edith had something to do with it, but Lissa, Marla Edith and I are only friends. Just friends, that's all. And Lissa, I don't mind telling you, that gets trying at times."

Brandon slid off the limb to stand before her in his brown trousers and tan shirt, unbuttoned at the collar. She could see the blood pulse at his neck.

"It's no secret to me, Brandon, Marla Edith trying to make claims on you. I understood about the job, building a room for her, at good wages, too."

She didn't tell him that she also worried if he'd compromised himself in some way, folks interpreting his driving with Marla Edith in her Buick as dating, getting in too deep. Marla Edith's tentacles reached farther than some people dared to think – her grip unyielding. She had heard that Marla Edith had even talked to a lawyer in Ozark about the Blue Vale School situation.

"Guess I'll have to have a talk with her. It could be true that she assumes too much, coming to White Oak Church when I preached." Brandon sighed in the hot wind.

"When Wardley preaches, too."

"Yes, Lissa, when Wardley preaches, too."

Lissa could sense that Brandon wanted to reach out and draw her to him. She was aware he realized what had happened that morning had taken its toll on her, too, as she was unable to mask the hurt in her eyes.

Lissa thought of the Bible School choir, Marla Edith under Brandon's feet. Volunteering to help him pass out the teachers' books and take roll – the young people's meetings Lissa had attended where Brandon and Marla Edith walked in together, her Buick parked outside.

"You must hate Wardley for sidetracking you, Brandon." She wanted to throw her arms around his neck. What was she thinking? She was engaged to Wardley, and he needed her.

"No," Brandon said, his voice, a vibrant bass. "Bewildered, yes. Confused, yes. I know he'll come to me and give me a fuller explanation. Really, I don't need one. I'm just an untrained Ozark-hillbilly who made a mistake getting interested in theology and philosophy the way I did."

CHAPTER NINETEEN

Wardley Stafford reared abruptly off his pillow, surprised that he'd dozed off. But he had to admit to himself that the blanket of guilt and depression had lifted. The fatigue, however, still hung like starlings over a manure pile, and he realized he needed a cup of strong coffee, but his thoughts of Lissa revived him. Wardley was glad he'd made a decision on the church problem. He concluded that it was indeed time for him and Lissa to finalize their plans.

He changed hastily into his youthful-looking blue suit. He hadn't realized it had grown so late. He slapped bay rum on his chin. Grabbing his smart boater hat, he stepped out and down the walk to the green Olds to head to the Massey farm. He straightened his shoulders, compensating for the fatigue he still felt.

Wardley reviewed in his mind that he had no church responsibilities that night. Fortunate. He pictured himself and Lissa at the furniture store picking out new kitchen linoleum. Strawberry ice cream sodas at the Rexall. Reviewing a few things about the earthquake-of-a-morning, making plans for our cozy future.

* * *

Lissa sat up, bewildered at first. Have I overslept? I do feel better, yet a heaviness weighs on me. It'll be better once Wardley explains the shocking event. Bewildering. So confusing. And Brandon, left hanging. Lissa straightened the quilted bedspread, poured water in her basin to freshen her face, then took her brush to catch a few blond strands that'd strayed. Believe I'll slip into my yellow voile. Thank God, Wardley will explain.

Reaching for her Bible on the nightstand, Lissa sat in the little sewing rocker, opening it to Psalm 37: "Commit thy way unto the Lord, trust also in him; and he shall bring it to pass."

Lissa bowed her head. Praying, she committed herself to God, asking for a blessing for Wardley, and that their meeting tonight would be blessed with understanding and grace.

Hearing the sound of a car door slam, she leaned to look out her white-curtained window. She smiled as she noticed Wardley unhooking the gate by the trumpet vine. How youthful he looks in the blue suit, swinging his straw boater like that. I do hope he got some rest, too.

Wardley sat by the oak stand table where Lissa had placed the tray with the snickerdoodle cookies, and the green-with-rosebud teapot and cups.

"The cookies are scrumptious, Lissa, and I always like the orange pekoe tea." Lissa could see his adoration for her as his eyes swept over her yellow dress. She seated herself in the oak rocker to his left and leaned forward.

"Glad the stressful episode of the morning is over, my dear. Yes, I can see already you feel better, too, Lissa." Wardley sipped his tea.

"Yes, Wardley, you – you said you'd try to...." Lissa waited for the explanation regarding Brandon being shoved aside. He said he would try to tell her the reason.

"Lissa, tell you what I think we ought to do. Get in the Olds tomorrow and drive over to Bradley's furniture store and pick out that linoleum for the kitchen. Have you decided on a color yet?"

"Wardley, no. Not tomorrow. We need to talk about this morning, the announcement you made that floored us all. You mentioned you would clear up some things for me, well, I ... I'm waiting." Lissa set her cup into the saucer on the stand table.

"Well, Lissa, churches sometimes have painful times. Decisions. Leaders in *my* position have to walk a fine line and make choices that may seem to hurt." He cleared his throat and brought his right fist to his mouth, then lowered it.

She recognized that Wardley was deliberately avoiding her. "Wardley, you need to know that this afternoon I drove over for a talk with Brandon. A long talk, in fact. I wanted his perspective on this. He won't contest your decision. But he is bewildered and hurt by you and the board jerking the rug out from under him." Lissa was surprised at the strength of her words. She noticed his eyes shift to the window, then back to her face.

"The Lord leads in strange ways. Strange ways sometimes, Lissa." Wardley adjusted his legs and straightened his back which had sagged. His mouth fell from a smile to a straight line.

His chest expanded as he breathed in, and his eyes narrowed. "Brandon? Brandon? What on earth can that man offer you? An Ozark hill farmer has nothing to offer a woman like you, Lissa." He looked at her as if he was a father lecturing a child. His eyes, hot rivets, beaded in on Lissa.

Lissa felt her own shoulders lift as if someone had struck her from behind. "You know, Wardley, I only want to understand. Have you explain–"

"Explain! Explain? Well, my dear, you know that men of my office have certain *confidences* to keep. I'm sure you understand – for the good of the church." He lifted his right leg over his left. He tried to look into her open blue eyes, but his eyes failed to hold their focus.

Lissa turned in her chair so that she could face him directly. Her heart surged. "Wardley, I'm beginning to conclude that you're deliberately avoiding my questions. You're hedging regarding your reasons for derailing Brandon." She noticed that her left hand trembled, nevertheless, her grip on her teacup was firm, and her eyes locked into his. She realized he probably thought she was pressuring him, maybe even thought, "It's the schoolteacher in her."

Wardley cleared his throat and took a deep breath. "The community here was misguided in attempting to select an untrained man like Fall. Church'll see the results when Nevins arrives. They'll be proud to have a man with his fine education."

"Wardley, the church made a decision. *You* supported it, even told Brandon so. What on earth made you change your mind? What happened? That's what I must know. I care about Brandon. We grew up together, we–"

"Lissa, Lissa, my dear, you must put it aside and not worry your–"

"Please, Wardley, don't call me 'dear' right now. I feel you're pushing me backwards. I'm not asking you to betray confidences, but please give me some idea."

This time Wardley shifted his left leg over his right one, his shoe dangling above a pink rose in the hooked rug. The movement of his ankle betrayed his growing anxiety and the precariousness of his predicament. He set his teacup on an end table, wiped his hand across his mouth, lips with an earlier gracious curve now flattened in a straight line. "You must trust me, Lissa. I love you. I simply cannot allow *our relationship* to suffer because of my duties."

"Duties? Trust? Wardley, I have to tell you," Lissa stood and moved directly in front of him. "I must tell you that I'm beginning to believe Brandon was sidetracked because of you. *You*, Wardley. It has to do with you. Something you wish to conceal." Lissa's legs trembled and her heart tried to leap into her throat.

"Me? Conceal? Sidetrack? How can you say those words, Lissa?" His voice took on a tinny quality, as if he thought she was unfairly accusing him – leaping over proper boundaries.

Lissa stepped closer, right arm holding her trembling left hand behind her arched back. "I'm also wondering if Rhutley Rennart had something to do with it."

Wardley swallowed, his eyes narrowed as if in pain. They searched the room, focusing at last on the picture of *The Gleaners* above the couch.

Lissa continued. "Yes. I do believe Rennart did, and you refuse to tell me." The clock ticked as she waited for his words.

Wardley looked as if he was beginning to feel like one of Lissa's scholars freshly directed to stand in the corner. He grunted and lifted himself awkwardly to his feet, towering a foot above her. His cheeks flushed, he raked one of his immaculately groomed hands through his splendid hair. "Lissa, my dear, you, you're unraveling our relationship, accusing me like that. You can't stand there and say–"

"I said it. Let it unravel, Wardley. Or, I should say, it's already unraveled."

"Lissa, you can't, you can't mean it – our love, our plans." His throat seemed to tighten as if it were as dry as the old well by the barn. His eyes widened, betraying his fear.

Lissa stepped over to reach for his straw boater on the coat rack. Skin on her ckeeks tightened as if she'd powdered her face with alum. Anger burn rose from her stomach to her breast.

"Wardley, I'm sorry, but I need to tell you that I cannot marry you. Perhaps we'll continue to be friends when this is over, but marriage–"

"Lissa. Lissa, my love. You *can't* say that. Tomorrow you'll see it differently. Things like this take time before they're understood. Don't say those words. I'll swing the Olds around tomorrow to drive you up to Springfield. Buy you a new fall suit."

"No, Wardley. I'm sorry, I'm hurt and I'm angry. Let me make myself clear again, I can't marry you. Good night, Wardley." She handed him the expensive cream-colored boater. His trembling hand grasped it by the rim.

Forgetting himself, he thrust it on his head at an awkward angle while still in the house. Eyes downcast, the powerful overseer of the Arkansas-Missouri church districts picked his way toward the front door, which Lissa held open for him. He attempted to lift back his shoulders as if to shift his fallen self-esteem and dignity to a respectable position. He staggered on toward his waiting new Olds, where he slid in on the plush seat, surrounded by luxury.

Lissa glanced out the window in the door as she choked back a sob, recognizing that Wardley's heart was a lonely place where a cold wind blew, even in an Ozark summer.

CHAPTER TWENTY

Marla Edith Maggler rolled out of bed at the first cock's crow. She tugged on her summer skirt in her attempts to ease it over her hips. She wouldn't waste time, right then, worrying over the added poundage. At her dressing table she brushed her hair, thankful that it still comported with the style and cut Cicily Woodburn had given her. She swiped her face with her powder puff and creamed her thick lips with hot red lipstick.

While checking her seams, she heard the shocking news on her radio about sheriff-shooter Clyde Barrow and that crazy girl named Bonnie Parker, who bounced around with him. She thought of Clyde's picture in the *Gazette*.

Young Barrow – a good-looking fellow. Had to admit it. Marla Edith hoped he stayed over in Oklahoma and away from the Branson Bank. She stuffed her feet into her white pumps.

The Buick eased along the gravel road. Meadowlarks rejoiced in the bright morning sunshine. At the Branson Bank, she pulled into a parking slot, bid her old Pap Sloan Maggler a quick good-bye. She sat for a while, watching him march through the door. Maggler turned the sign on the inside of the bank door to "Open."

Nine o'clock and life seemed to hang. A copper-colored hound loped across the street, rear end dragging to one side. Rains had stopped, yet people prayed they'd start again. Farmers still had hopes for a fall harvest. One lonely white cloud drifted above Inspiration Point. A layer of mist rose up from White River valley.

Marla Edith checked her purse to see if she had change enough for coffee and scrambled eggs over at the Red Onion Cafe. Nelda Davis, who slung hash and waited tables, might catch her up on the local news. And that was some news – Lissa Massey cutting Reverend Wardlcy Stafford loose, way the rumors had it.

"You gonna have the Baldknob Special?" Nelda dug the nail of her index finger into her mop of hair while smacking her gum.

Marla Edith pondered a moment, her brown eyes surveying the menu. "What is the Baldknob Special, Nelda?"

"Scrambled eggs 'n toast. Jelly goes with it. Java included. That's twenty cents. Want the bacon, then the price is twenty-five cents." Nelda licked the point of her lead pencil.

Marla hesitated, then said, "I'll take the Special." She realized that a roll of fat did show at her waist. But then the way cotton goods drew up these days, it didn't necessarily mean she was wider in girth, did it?

"You like your Java black, Marla?" Nelda poured. Her gum popped.

"I'll take it black this morning, Nelda. Gotta be ready for what the day throws at me." She chuckled in her low, earthy chuckle.

The breakfast turned out to be boring, having to sit there and eat the strawberry jam on her toast and pop the crisp bacon into her mouth while listening to Nelda run down President Roosevelt and his homely wife with the big buckteeth up there in Washington D.C.

"I'm against the CCC, and the WPA too, Marla. Yep, my pa says you can't even find a hand to fork hay in the valley these days, men knowing they can get a bigger check with them government agencies and not have to work. You seen them leanin on their shovels, ain't you?"

What bothered Marla Edith was Nelda's next comment.

"You know, Ceedie Snow told me that Brandon Fall, the starved-to-death-looking man from over the hill who wants to be a preacher, is going into the CCC. Well, with two hundred thousand out-o-work men leaping on the freight trains these days, he might as well."

"No, I hadn't heard about it." Marla Edith wiped her mouth with her paper napkin. Why hadn't Brandon told her? She had a whole upstairs that needed remodeling.

Then Nelda wanted to know if Marla Edith was keeping up with the Little Orphan Annie column in the funnies. "Leapin' lizards," Nelda said, "that youngun sure knows how to keep ahead of the freight train. Her and her Daddy Warbucks."

After Marla Edith popped the last of the bacon in her mouth, she took out her compact and touched up her lips, walked over to the register to pay Nelda her twenty-five cents plus the two mills tax.

By ten thirty, Marla Edith had visited Vern's Dime Store, buying herself one of the gold-toned compacts on sale for thirty-nine cents. Next, she slid the hangers back and forth on the racks at Clementine's Women's Wear, but she decided she'd wait and see what Clementine brought in for her fall line.

When Marla Edith looped back again on South Main, she let up on the gas pedal, staring at the decrepit Model T in the lot at Pempton's Used Cars. Brandon in town? Got his old jalopy started after all.

She parked in front of the cement watering trough, now dirt-filled and overgrown with weeds. Sure enough – through the dusty window, there hunched Brandon in the office with Melvin Pempton. Brandon going to trade cars?

Marla Edith debated whether or not she should barge on in, then decided that she could offer advice and at least give Brandon support. Never knew what crafty Melvin might try to put over on a sensitive man like Brandon. Probably a good thing he got derailed from that tacky little preaching job anyway.

"Why, Brandon, fancy meeting you here. Unloading the tin Lizzie?"

Brandon's shoulders slumped as he scanned the penciled figures on the paper Melvin shoved before him. He straightened as Marla Edith sashayed through the door. "Marla Edith. You in town this time of the day? Well, yeah, finally trading in the old T."

"Now ain't we got some *real* help? Howdy, Miss Maggler. Lucky dog. Now we got the loan officer's *daughter* here to help us, Brandon." Melvin chuckled. He shot Marla Edith a wink. Her red-nailed hand reached out to rest on the back of Brandon's shoulder.

"Have a seat, Miss Marla. Sell you that yellow LaSalle out there under the locust." A sultry grin spread across Melvin's face.

"I bet you would, Melvin. No, I'll just sit here by Brandon to see that you don't steal his socks." She laughed, then winked at Melvin.

"Fall, I'm a gonna give you twenty-five dollars for your Model T out there. Your arm about broke from trying to get it started, ain't it? Tires all patched and bald."

Brandon shifted his long legs and pinched his nostrils as if he'd caught the drift of Marla Edith's musky perfume. Her arm crept behind Brandon's chair as she leaned closer.

"Well, what'll be the difference?" Brandon lifted his head in order to glance again at the shiny used Model A outside the dust-streaked window.

"Best deal I can give you, and I'm a telling you, the best deal anyone'll get today, four hundred fifty dollars. But Fall, I'm a gonna need forty dollars down."

Melvin sat back, his orange tie with the coffee stains askew on a shirt already dark with sweat circles under his arms.

"Why, Brandon, that sounds like a real good deal. Car like that at that price? That's not much down, either. Forty dollars." Marla Edith patted Brandon's shoulder, face near his, which drew down in worry or doubt.

"Keys in the car. You and Miss Maggler climb in that green Ford and take her for a spin over on the slab." Melvin winked his left eye again at Marla Edith.

"Good idea, Brandon. Let's try it out. See how it drives down the slab towards Hollister." Brandon's shoulders slumped, his face fell, betraying agony over the money – the penciled figures.

* * *

"It doesn't drive like your Buick, Marla Edith, but it holds the road pretty well and the engine doesn't seem to heat up. Yes, I believe it's a good car. Like to drive it home for Pa and Ma. Nearly broke my back and arm on that Model T this morning. Forty dollars down?"

Back at the shack-of-an-office, Melvin tapped his pencil with tobacco-stained fingers as if time was running out. He licked his lips and leered at Marla Edith.

Brandon leaned back in his chair, his eyes narrowing for the close. "Tell you what, Melvin." He cleared his throat. "I can go with four-hundred dollars on the Ford. Worked out on time payments. Take away the twenty-five for my Model T. You say you got to have forty dollars down? Today?" Brandon's eyebrows furrowed.

Marla Edith noticed how Brandon looked away like he was searching for a bull frog in a dry gulch. She knew he wondered: *Where will I ever get forty dollars?*

Melvin honed in. "Tell you what, Mr. Fall." He nudged Brandon's shoulder with a knuckle. "You just made me an offer I can go with. Four hundred dollars, minus the Model T. Best deal you'll get in the whole state." Melvin winked at Marla Edith. His wily grin spread at the surge of sales success.

Brandon glanced over at Marla Edith, eyes shining as if she were about to climb on the Ferris wheel with him. Her lips parted. It wasn't news to her that Brandon Fall wouldn't have forty dollars. Who on earth in the whole county would these days?

"Let's step outside for a chat, Brandon." Marla Edith leaped to her feet. She grabbed his arm and dragged him to the door, her heels scraping the floor.

"No way I can come up with that kind of down payment, Marla Edith. The Model T has to be junked. I need a car to get Pa over to the doctor at Ozark. I can't go away with them stranded out there."

Marla could see that depression weighed on him and that he hadn't yet rebounded from his pulpit derailment at White Oak. Maybe she could help lift the pall of poverty from his lean shoulders. Lean though he was, there was an athletic look about him that, well....

"Brandon, I just thought of something." Marla Edith's eyes widened like a spider noticing a hesitating fly.

Brandon dug the toe of his scarred brogue in the dust.

"You know the forty dollars from Bible School? The offering you wanted me to send to Cousin J. Moody?" Marla leaned forward.

"Well, yes, but that money's for–"

"I never got around to sending it yet." Marla Edith dipped her head in mock apology. "We'll get it there this fall. I can write out a check for the forty dollars. You got twenty acres of soy beans by Dodie Creek, haven't you? Cash crop? Beans not all dried up like last year."

"What are you saying? Bible School money? Pay it back in the fall? Then you'll send it on to Africa? Two more months? Why, Marla Edith." Brandon's eyes were wide saucers.

She, seeing his hanging mouth, simpered. "Just a few weeks, Brandon." A smile sliced across her face.

"*No*, Marla Edith. *No*, that just wouldn't be the right thing to do. You go on and get that check out to the mission. Right away. Besides, the July rain may not come." His brow wrinkled.

"Brandon, listen to me." Her fingers pinched his biceps. "This is your opportunity to get a car you can drive up to Springfield to take a Bible class this fall. Think of it. Think of it as the Lord's will. Be serious, now." Marla's lips drew into a pious line.

"No, Marla Edith, No."

In spite of his no, Marla Edith drew back her shoulders and beamed.

* * *

Late that evening, hearing the gravel spinning, Serena looked up from her porch chair. "Why, I declare, Owney. Here comes Brandon driving a real good green Ford. I wonder how he arranged that?" Her face wreathed in a big smile. It was evident now that her son would never again have to jack up the Model T and risk breaking his arm trying to crank it.

Brandon climbed out of the now dusty Model A. He dragged toward the house, head bent, hands in the pockets of his worn overalls.

My, don't he look sad? Serena thought.

CHAPTER TWENTY-ONE

Brilliant sunlight highlighted the green in the trees, the grass, and the young corn in the valley fields. Estra smiled when she looked out across the field that sloped toward White River and saw the corn, blades stretching. Won't it be a blessing if the rains come late summer, and we have a corn crop this year?

But those two other matters hadn't at all been a blessing. No. Felt more like a death in the family, Brandon Fall getting derailed. Lissa sending Wardley Stafford scooting.

Estra thought of poor Serena and Owney. How worn out they were, waiting for windows of hope in their lives only to have such a promising one slammed shut.

Aunt Gustie, who'd walked over to help her bake bread, kneaded dough, then divided it for the loaf pans.

Through the kitchen window Gustie could see Lissa in the garden furiously attacking the weeds in the green bean rows. "How long has she been out there?" She turned to Estra.

"Gets up before the sun comes up over the ridge. Slips on a work dress and out she goes. You ought to see the blisters on her hands. Attacks those weeds like she's killing snakes. Working through letting Reverend Stafford go." Estra reached for a long-handled mixing spoon.

"I was to blame, at least partially." Aunt Gustie's chin, stony as Mount Branson cliffs. "I laughed and joked and egged Lissa on. I never gave her no caution, Estra. I gotta share part of the blame."

"We were overpowered with Wardley Stafford's position, who he is among us. Such a fine-looking man at his age, widower needing a companion. And these hard times. Lissa really was fond of him. She'll work it through." Estra cleared her throat.

"Well, Brandon's been over here every night. Them sittin out there on the front porch, walkin down to the Dodie Creek bridge. Guess she'll have to tighten the screws to keep him out of the CCC after him getting dumped like that." Gustie scraped flour into her hands with a table knife.

"Lissa tells me he didn't make it over to the CCC office yet. I guess his car's still sitting up on those blocks. Anyway, she encouraged him to apply for a scholarship up at that St. Mark Seminary in Kansas City where Reva's husband graduated." Estra brushed her cheek with her arm, thankful for Gustie's help with the bread baking.

"Think Marla Edith'll keep coming to White Oak with Brandon derailed and Stafford over at Reeds Spring now?" Gustie asked.

"Well, I doubt it, but I'll tell you what I heard Marla Edith say, once." Estra stepped over to the dry sink to wash flour and dough from her hands. "She told me once that 'wherever there's a pot, there's a lid that fits.'" Gustie bent over, cackled, and showed her near-toothless gums.

Estra allowed herself a big smile. "Sounds just like her. The poor girl – er, woman – is lonely. Sometimes I feel sorry for her. Gustie, we need to pray for Marla Edith."

"Well, I'll tell you one thing, Estra Massey. You know that old Dutch oven of mine? Nine years ago I had to throw away the lid. Cracked right down the middle. Well, I ain't ever been able to find no lid that'll exactly fit that pot." Their laughter echoed in the kitchen.

* * *

Aunt Gustie limped out onto the side porch to sit in the willow rocker to think about Brandon and Lissa. She took her paring knife and sliced an apple through to the core, then, turning it, she chopped across the slices. She lifted the apple to her leathery lips and sliced off a mouthful. Her chin rose and fell as she chewed.

As Gustie gummed her apple, she thought about the forty dollars in the Prince Albert tobacco box under her bed. She decided right then she would soon have Lissa take her in to dentist, Vilus Litlock, next week. Get them new store-teeth. Yep. Next week. Gustie grinned.

* * *

Brandon didn't walk over that evening. He drove over, gravel spitting beneath the wheels of his new Ford, face spread in a wide grin, left arm hanging out the driver's side window.

"Wonder who that is?" Lissa asked. When the car got close enough to the yard fence, she recognized the driver. "I don't believe it. Brandon, where did you get it? When?" Lissa leaped from the porch steps to race toward him.

"Surprised? Yes, well, er, finally able to unload the tin Lizzie. It rusted out, and you know I nearly busted my back trying to get it started." Brandon grinned widely.

Lissa realized this was no time to inquire about how the Falls, or Brandon himself, for that matter, could afford to trade cars this year, even for a used one.

"After we take our walk, Lissa, I'll drive you into Branson to the Palace for ice cream. I do want your approval on my Model A." He grinned, taking her arm and guiding her toward the pasture path that led to the woods beyond.

"Sunset's beautiful over Inspiration Point this evening, isn't it, Brandon?"

"Yes, Lissa, yes, the summer sunsets are spectacular. One of the ways God comes to us, through beauty." Though he didn't say it, his face revealed that he thought that Lissa was surely classed among the beautiful and her heart filled with the love of God.

They strolled together on the old logging road through the hickories behind the Massey cornfield. Rufus, tail wagging, trotted ahead to warn them if there were any snakes.

"I love Mayapple plants, Brandon. Look at them. Fruit ripening yellow like that. So glossy and waxy, one wonders if they're real."

Brandon, clasping Lissa's hand, led her to the wide log just close enough to Dodie Creek so that they could hear the murmuring water, near the spot where the spring mushrooms grow, when the rains come in April. "Lissa, we've both been hit hard these last weeks."

"Yes, Brandon, we've both suffered." She squeezed his big rough hand.

"Do you believe God uses suffering for our good, Lissa? I do. My old friend whose works I keep reading believes so."

"Who is that, Brandon?" A whippoorwill called to its mate.

"Søren. Søren Kierkegaard. Quite a name, isn't it? Danish. Name means 'Church yard.' Died about a hundred years ago." Brandon shifted his legs to avoid a nettle.

"Suffering and pain help us sort out what's important, don't they, Brandon? Maybe they have a holy use." Why did I turn from him? I always loved him. How could I have doubted his love? Lissa's thoughts pressed at her mind.

"Yes, Lissa. Yes. Søren believed if we don't run from suffering but stay with it, sooner or later, we'll see the face of Christ."

Lissa felt the completeness between them. Whatever it was that night that had separated them had vanished. In time, she would ask him about it. A cooling wind touched their necks, and the willow boughs above them swayed.

Lissa, in her blue shirtwaist, lifted her face to his, noting the light in his dark-brown eyes and the way his hair curled and fell over his forehead.

"Brandon, the hard times will end some day. We have to keep faith and hope … we.…"

"Lissa," he released her hand and placed his hand around her waist. "Lissa, something I have to ask you."

In the distance, a whippoorwill answered the call of the one by the creek bank.

"Yes, Brandon. What is it?"

"Lissa, I have nothing. No material goods to offer you. Yet I believe God has a plan for us, you and me. Together. Lissa, my darling, marry me."

Her blue eyes opened, her face radiant in the evening light. Sweetness of ripe blackberries perfumed the wind about them.

"Yes. Brandon, yes. My first love, yes."

He bent his sunburned face and pressed his lips against her waiting ones.

They held one another while the sun slid behind Inspiration Point, and a cardinal sang, blessing them with his "Sweet cheer, sweet cheer."

When she could speak, Lissa reached up to hold his chin, feeling the dark-whiskered sandpaper and strength of his lean face.

"God blesed you with much more than material things, Brandon. He gave you a fine mind and the abilities to be a minister. You'll see. I have faith. When this depression passes, you will be amazed at the doors that will open for you."

"There is faith in your voice, my love."

"Faith and hope in my heart. In your heart too, Brandon, or you wouldn't have asked me to marry you."

"Yes. It's because of the hope and love and faith. Eternal things, aren't they? It's because of them that I'm able to ask you to be my wife."

CHAPTER TWENTY-TWO

Marla Edith perched on the edge of a small oak chair before her open bedroom window. She reached down to smooth her silk hose over her calves, straightening the seams.

Whoooeee. The heat. Wonder how Brandon Fall's soy beans and corn are doing on the lower twenty? This heat'd burn the fur off a squirrel's tail.

She held her newly-polished nails before her, hoping their luster would hold up at least two weeks. Marla Edith recognized that few of the women, young or old, in these hills had either money or time to paint their nails. With Brandon Fall getting dumped over at the White Oak Church and with Reverend Stafford hightailing it down to Reeds Spring to help with the installation of a new pastor and staying on to teach a class, Marla Edith guessed she might just go back to the town church in Branson.

And that's another thing. Lissa Massey cutting the Reverend loose like that. Well, Wardley Stafford found out how those Masseys kept commitments, didn't he? She chuckled, recalling the movie she and Brandon had seen that day they gave his second-hand Model A a trial, speeding all the way up the slab to Ozark.

Well, yes, Brandon had protested, said he didn't have change to spare to go to a movie. But when she saw the marquee over the Valentine Theater: *It Happened One Night*, starring Claudette Colbert and Clark Gable, she'd dug in her purse. "I've got thirty cents, Brandon. Enough for both of us."

A BRANSON LOVE

Sitting in the plush red seats watching the enchanting movie, Brandon did admit his anxiety over swapping cars had vanished. He stretched out his legs, head straining forward, as the miraculous pictures flicked across the silver screen.

Brandon hadn't told her, but by the way he lifted his head and grinned, she could tell it was the first movie he'd seen.

That afternoon, Marla Edith decided to leave thirty minutes early to go pick up Pa at the bank. Time for a cherry phosphate at the Rexall on a hot afternoon like this. Marla Edith smiled, thinking of how Twili Shorts at the Rexall kept up on the latest news.

* * *

"I got it from Nelda across the street in the cafe," Twili said as she placed the cherry phosphate in front of Marla Edith, who perched in the little wire chair with the valentine heart wire loops.

"You don't mean Lissa Massey when you said 'that blonde,' do you, Twili?" Marla Edith tipped her phosphate and a slip of foam ran over the edge.

"Who else? Nelda said she's engaged to that good-looking Brandon Fall who rattled in over at Melvin's in that backfiring tin Lizzie, and drove off in a green used Model A last week." She smacked her Doublemint and waited for Miss Marla Maggler's reaction.

"That whippersnap ... she stole my...." Then Marla Edith realized that she absolutely could not afford to blow up at the Rexall with Carna Harnack and Bernidene Buttle dipping chocolate ice cream with those little bitty spoons at the table across from her.

Marla Edith drew on her phosphate straw, mouth puckered, her eyes turning dark and cold like the big pool in White River where it runs deep under Buford's Bluff.

* * *

"This is the third time this week you driving me into town and staying the day," Sloan Maggler said, who recognized his olive-skinned daughter was more than ordinarily flustered. She'd applied that new Mum deodorant from that little jar, but already her dress showed sweat stains under her arms.

    Marla Edith realized that Pa Maggler's stomach growled over her going on thirty-one and no reasonable prospects. Well, yes, she'd been fooling around, laughing and pushing the shoulder of that hillbilly, Brandon, over on that rock pile. "But shoot, he's not gonna amount to anything, just another country preacher," he'd told her.

    Marla Edith knew he preferred a businessman like Melvin Pempton for a son-in-law, one who was willing to wallow for success, even if it had to be with used cars in desperate times like these.

    Besides, he'd told Marla Edith that she took after him – a little hardheaded. Old Sloan chuckled as he eyed the dried-up corn rattling in the blast of wind, as if wondering if there would soon be some farm foreclosures coming up.

    Marla Edith bit her lips in silence. She gripped the ivory wheel of the Buick and ground her teeth. She couldn't get the Masseys out of her mind – they and their laughable names. *Estra*, sounded like a laxative, and that eighth-grader, *Slade*, who, she was reluctant to admit, had a good brain and, so far, behaved reasonably. Nothing like his faded blond sister with her pious face, and her ridiculous old aunt, what's-her-name. *Gut-sie*?

    Well, anyway, that Lissa'd just have to live down the embarrassment she caused her family and the whole White Oak Church when her brain weakened and she got herself engaged to Reverend Wardley Stafford. Up and cut him loose faster than if she'd been fishing on Dodie Creek and had a nasty snapping turtle on her hook.

    Sloan Maggler closed the Buick door, sauntering on across the sidewalk to the bank. Marla Edith backed out of the parking space with a roar, wheels pitching gravel. She shifted, glanced in her rearview mirror, and made an illegal U-turn.

    Brandon was bound to drive in today. Marla Edith had a few words for Brandon Fall after hearing he was engaged to that skinny, immature Lissa. Let him sweat over the forty dollars. Looks like everybody's corn and soy beans dried up.

    Oughta call Brandon, but of course, the Falls were too poor for a phone. She'd have driven over to his tacky place, but she didn't want to risk a tangle with old lady Serena in front of his sick pa.

Then Marla Edith remembered that on Saturdays Serena sent Brandon lumbering into Branson to market her pitiful crate of eggs.

Marla Edith sweltered in the Buick, waiting at the side of Slavanskie's Produce. While wiping the sweat from underneath her dress collar with her handkerchief, she spied Brandon pushing open the screen door, sauntering on toward his dusty Model A, pocketing the measly egg money.

"Brandon. Over here." Marla Edith stood by her open car door and waved, her best smile spreading across her face, lips refurbished in new red. She hated that the *Mum* had broken down.

"Why, Marla Edith. Yes. Well, er...." Brandon hesitated. Seeming to realize he couldn't ignore her, he stepped around the side of the produce shack to her car parked under the shade of a hackberry.

"Brandon. Where have you been? If you'd have had a phone, I'd have called you." She concluded it was best to start slowly, keep the anger down below the belt for now. "Have a seat in the shade here."

Brandon slid in on the passenger side with reluctance, as if torn over how to break the news. "Marla Edith, I, uh, you probably heard that Lissa Massey and I are engaged and plan–"

Marla turned to face him, her knee touching his, corners of her mouth turning down, her eyes narrowing.

"Yes. I heard. I heard. You have the nerve to sit there and tell me that? Engaged? Brandon Fall, you engaged to that...." The burning ball of anger below her belt burst into tongues of fire that lapped up around her throat.

"How could you, Brandon Fall? After *our* relationship? After all I did for you? You spending hours with me? Me saving the Bible school by directing the chorus." Marla Edith reveled in seeing the shock in Brandon's face as it paled. Her black eyes stared daggers as his chest heaved and the pulse quickened at his neck.

"Marla Edith, yes, it's true. You offered to give me work and paid me a good salary. We took some drives together." His eyes cut to the side as if he had old memories of how she put her hand behind his neck and fingered his hair. "But we, we're just friends. That's all, good friends."

"Friends? Friends?" Her brow furrowed and her eyes bulged. "I came over to every one of your sermons." *That ought to make him feel guilty.*

"Hold yourself, Marla Edith. Now, it was you who decided to come to White Oak Church to hear me preach." Brandon stared straight into her eyes.

Marla Edith realized she'd better shove the anger back down and try another tack if she wanted to stay in control.

"You'll ruin your life, Brandon. Throw it away." That's right, expose the twerp, Lissa's, deficiencies, and emphasize my good points. Her face flushed. "Besides, I saved the Bible School for you, Brandon, and...."

"Marla Edith, I-I can't let you … you're a good director of childrens' choirs, yes. But the deacons asked you, I didn't. I really can't let you–" Brandon's face reddened, his lips puckered at the corners.

"Let me? Let me? Brandon Fall, I'll say what I choose to say. You listen to me." Her breath rasped, and her lips curled as though she was sucking on a green persimmon. Struggling, she twisted her olive-toned face into a smile as she put her hot palm on his thigh to make her point. Her smile wavered like heat on concrete through the pain in her eyes.

"I have so much more to offer you, Brandon. Go somewhere, you and me. Someday I inherit Mother's farm. You know what kind of buildings are on *that* farm. Not a pile of rocks and lean-to buildings like that forty you sit on. What do you want? Seminary? I can find–"

"Marla Edith, Marla Edith, please take your hand off my leg. I'm sorry you misunderstood our friendship–"

"*Misunderstood*? After what we've been through together? The way I paid you? Misunderstood? Arranging that down payment for your tacky little Model A. You've got nerve, Brandon Fall, and wanting to be a preacher?"

Hurl a few insults. He needed them. Yes, it felt good to let the anger boil over. Let it scorch and wither him into being the laughingstock of the community.

"Again, Marla Edith – I didn't ask for the money. *You* practically shoved it on me. Besides, why did you delay so in sending it?"

She backed up to gain traction so she could plow in again. "Listen, Brandon." She tucked her finger under her dress collar and shook her hair. "I know you're half-blind now. I'm not stupid, I understand that. You've been through an embarrassing situation, being rejected over at the church. Lissa's bound to try to take advantage of you. You know she stole my school from under me, and her scholars didn't actually *win* that trophy–"

"Stop it, Marla Edith. I can't allow you to run Lissa down. You're accusing her falsely." The color rose in Brandon's cheeks. His eyes narrowed.

She gasped as the second roll of anger hit her. Her eyes, hot rivets. "Get out. Get out of my car, Brandon Fall. You two-timer-no-guts-preacher-failure. You deserve to be cut loose from opportunities I offer. When you see the mistake of it, don't come crawling back to me like Lissa did to you, mewing and sniveling." Her contempt boiled like bitter gall.

By then Brandon was already out of the Buick, closing the door. "Good-bye, Marla Edith." His voice wobbled as if he realized the stumbling words were impoverished. Insufficient.

Marla Edith glared at him, head bent, shoulders sagging. Sweat dripping. His hands trembled as he stumbled toward his car. Marla Edith's shrieks pierced the air.

"You fool! I want my forty dollars and I want it today." Her face, a scalded pig's head, leered out the open window. "You'll live to regret this day, Brandon Fall." The wind caught her words, whipping them around his red, wilting ears.

"And another thing, Brandon Fall, I never gave that slouchy Lissa Massey *any* message that night you were on the way to the hospital and had the gall to flag me down. I drove out of my way up their long lane, praying I wouldn't get my Buick hung up on a rock. That whole Massey outfit was out in the chicken house. Looked like bumbling Russian peasants. Never heard such squawking. You think I wanted chicken manure on my new pumps? I just hit the gas and hightailed it right on out the lane."

Then Brandon knew. Lissa. Lissa waited for me that night. "Oh, dear Lord," he began to pray.

CHAPTER TWENTY-THREE

Brandon forked in his breakfast of fresh eggs and golden topped biscuits while Serena sipped black coffee from a chipped cup at the table with him. "You're worn out, Brandon. These times, they're wearing us all thin." Her hand trembled as she set the cup onto the saucer.

"Don't worry about me, Mother. Going to stroll through the corn and make a decision about it. Probably have to leave it stand, or cut it for fodder. Have to wonder if the cattle'll even eat it." His sad eyes focused on the crack in the wall that zigzagged upwards from behind the squat kitchen range. He lingered a while as if his thoughts were arranging the words: I'm headed for disaster.

"We still have milk and eggs, and the hogs, Brandon. We won't starve. Better times'll come. You'll see."

Brandon held back from telling her of the shame and guilt weighing on his heart like a sour miasma over a swamp.

After breakfast, he grabbed a hickory walking-stick and headed out through the miserable stalks of dried-up corn and soy beans. Better turn the cattle in and let them graze. Not enough nubbins even to think of husking it.

While he stumbled through the dry stalks, his shame about Marla Edith continued its smouldering burn like the dump by the slough.

But she's not fully responsible. I am. I was the one half-blinded, stumbling along. Why didn't I see? He could scarcely endure his thoughts.

"Forty dollars. Forty dollars." He mumbled as the wind rattled dried corn stalks. "Maybe I should take the Model A back to Melvin."

But Brandon knew if he did that, Serena would have to depend on the neighbors to get Owney to the doctor in Ozark.

"I'd be reduced to riding a lop-eared mule," he mumbled, struggling for answers.

* * *

That evening, Brandon heard a car rattling up the lane. A cloud of dust settled as it parked by the scrub oak outside. He rose from the porch step and headed through the burnt-up grass for the gate to greet two White Oak Church deacons, Silas Whitsitt and Rhutley Rennart. *Lord, help me to be cordial to Rhutley Rennart.* "Hello, neighbors." His hand raked through his hair.

"Why, uh, hello, Brother Fall." Deacon Whitsitt cleared his throat while he looked down at his work-scarred shoes. "Brother Rennart and I have a matter we want to go over with you."

I wonder if they're going to ask me to preach until Elwin gets here. That'd take nerve. Brandon locked his hands together over the top of his bib overalls.

"Why don't you jest come out here by the car, Brandon, and we'll take a look at the matter," Deacon Whitsitt urged.

They gathered as the evening sun turned orange, then red through the dust over the western hills. Brother Rennart unfolded a letter from his bib overall pocket.

"Ahemmm. Brother Fall, we want you to take a look at this letter from Brother J. Moody Maggler. Letter all the way from the African Mission."

Brandon's heart chilled. *Now what?* He raked his hand through his hair as he leaned to scan the page in his hand.

Cousin Marla Edith Maggler wrote saying that a Bible School offering was lifted for our mission. We rejoiced as we need the money as well as your prayers. However, I have to inform you that after quite a delay, I have not received the money.

A pain rushed up Brandon's side as his heart knocked and heat flushed his cheeks. A bitter gall crept to the back of his tongue. Marla Edith. No. She didn't?

Then he recognized that in her desperation, Marla Edith's wrath would be unchecked. Humiliated and shamed, she'd gone to the congregation.

"Need you to give us an explanation, Brother Fall. What happened to that offering?" Rhutley Rennart leaned back as he stuffed the letter into his bib overall pocket.

How can I say it? The painful thoughts surfaced. Any way the words come out of my mouth, it'll look like I'm blaming Marla Edith or excusing myself. "Yes. It's true. The offering was for Reverend Maggler's African Mission." Brandon cleared his throat as he wondered, should I invite them up to the porch?

"Did you send it? Maybe it got lost in the mail, going all the way to Africa?" Silas Whitsitt's wrinkled face showed a genuine concern for the obviously suffering young man.

"I know this may be contested, but Marla Edith took the offering. She personally volunteered to send it to her cousin, emphasizing that she had the correct address. I ... I'll have to talk to her about this."

"Well, Brother Fall, it's a bit late, ain't it? Being's we done checked with Sister Maggler and she said that you spent the forty dollars on that Ford parked yonder. Forty dollars for the down payment." Rennart gloated as if he'd just nailed a possum hide to a board to dry.

A desert wind howled in Brandon's brain. He caught himself by a lean arm on Rennart's car. *Oh, Lord, how far have I fallen?* Brandon wiped cold sweat from his forehead.

"We're going to require a confession, Brandon. A confession in front of the church. And it looks like Miss Maggler ain't going to be sending any money. Guess you'll have to sell something here at the farm." Rennart nodded to the gunmetal-green Model A.

* * *

"I hope Marla Edith doesn't take it out on Slade in school this year. All this animosity and bitterness." Lissa clasped Brandon's hand as they leaned against the wide trunk of the white oak in her yard.

"It's another tight rope, Lissa. Way we try to work it out will determine it, won't it?" They'd gone over it, she and Brandon, the sorry, boiling mess. Lissa hadn't rejected him or stepped back, Brandon concluded as warmth enfolded his heart.

"I witnessed it. Brandon, though I was concerned when Marla Edith volunteered to send the money, I didn't say anything. I thought you'd keep tabs on it." A worried frown creased Lissa's brow, a sudden wind whipped the collar of her yellow calico.

"How can you respect me, Lissa, if I have to walk up in front of the congregation and try to explain it, begging their pardon?" He looked across to the shrinking pasture pond and the dried-up cattails.

Lissa noticed that Aunt Gustie had come out to hang the upstairs curtains, which she'd volunteered to launder, on the line behind them. Aunt Gustie had been so deferring since the Wardley Stafford situation and Lissa's broken engagement to him.

Was Gustie eavesdropping? Leaning her ear across the washline? Lissa glanced back at Aunt Gustie.

"I've taken a job, starting Monday, over at Alf Fenwick's place helping him clear scrub oak and blackberry briars from that ten acres that joins up against Route 65. Pay me fifty cents a day. Build muscle and put a little money in my pocket. But forty dollars?" His voice faded.

"I can save it out of my teaching salary, Brandon, but it'll take six months with our bills as they are. I can ask Mother for it, but–"

"No, Lissa, I can't allow it. No. I'll handle it. Another thing. I've been too reluctant to confront that pompous Stafford over how he betrayed me." Brandon shifted his lanky body as he noticed a cicada laboriously climbing the rough bark of the tree. "Live and learn, Lissa. I thought being a Christian meant one absorbed everything. Well, I've concluded that there are certain things one can't let fly past, within oneself and with others. I'm going to confront him. I want to hear Wardley's own explanation. I'd have had a job and salary if it hadn't been for him."

"I'll support you, Brandon." Lissa realized she, herself, had been too passive, absorbing it all. Wardley's power had threatened and silenced their tongues, made them susceptible and deferring. There were times when it was appropriate to say, "Whoa, there," and, "I believe you owe me an explanation about that."

The wind shifted, announcing autumn in the air. Already the leaves on the black-trunked ash across the yard were turning yellow. Overhead, a giant flock of geese in V formation flew southward. The wind carried drifts of dried grasses and scorched corn leaves.

"We'll get through it, Brandon. We have to do what's right. Remember your sermon: 'The Lord is at hand.' We won't do it in our own strength. I had to face my situation, Brandon, when Wardley betrayed you, and in a way, all of us." She patted his warm hand.

"You had courage, Lissa. I'm proud of you, and I know it caused you pain and worry."

They looked at each other as simultaneously the words came to their lips – "All things work together for good to them that love God, to them who are the called according to his purpose."

* * *

Old Gustie limped across Dodie Creek bridge. "O Lord, O Lord," she mumbled. "I ain't been no good. Not goin to services regular. Puttin up excuses. Old backslider's what I am." Her hickory-colored calico skirt whipped about her lean shanks as her hard heels hit the boards.

Bursting into her log cottage, old Gustie, favoring her sore foot, hobbled over to her bed covered with the Log Cabin patchwork quilt.

"Clunk." Her hard knees hit the even harder floor. "I'm a gettin too old fer this. Gotta find another place to keep my money."

There it was – her Prince Albert tobacco can. She emptied it into her lap and began to sort out her forty dollars, change in one pile, dollar bills in another. Her thin lips moved as she mumbled, "Thirty-eight, thirty-nine, forty...."

CHAPTER TWENTY-FOUR

Brandon's heart knocked at his ribs as he reached up to rap on the white-painted door of the parsonage beside the brick church in Reeds Spring. "Worth it, using the gas to get this over with," he mumbled.

His knees trembled, his mouth dry as a sandstone in the sun. His Adam's apple bobbed as he tried to swallow.

Brandon was surprised when Wardley Stafford, blue-striped shirt unbuttoned at the collar, opened the door, eyes widening when he saw him.

"Why, Fall, er, ah, *Brother* Brandon. What a surprise. Yes. Yes." His fingers toyed with his thick hair.

Brandon stared at Wardley's eyes and knew that Stafford didn't think he'd have the gumption to actually drive this far to face him.

Brandon also recognized that Wardley Stafford's years were beginning to etch his spirit, like the rain grooved those old yellow rocks by Dodie Creek bridge. Myrna dying. Lissa Massey cutting him off, trouble with the White Oak folks, necks unevenly yielding to his yoke.

"Why, come on in the office, Brother Fall. By the way, you interested in preaching on a circuit? Have to drive back and forth between three little hill churches, but a good chance...."

Now he's offering me one of those backwoods churches, twenty, thirty people. Baptize out in the creek. Brandon realized Wardley Stafford was attempting to pacify him. Stafford seated himself in the swivel office chair behind a desk, *Young's Concordance* spread open on it.

Brandon seated himself in the straight chair underneath the picture of Jesus knocking at a big, arched wooden door. No, after that Sunday, he didn't expect warm hospitality here. "Brother Stafford, there're some things I have to tell you. That is, er–"

"Why, yes, son. Yes. Expect so. Young man with your abilities." Stafford reached for his glasses. "Want a character reference letter for the government? Entering the CCC?" He drew his massive fist to his mouth and attempted to swallow.

"I've considered it, President Roosevelt's Conservation Corps, but I did find a local job." Brandon's hard muscle-over-bone from chopping brush and scrub oak held his frame in the chair so he didn't bolt. He felt his already sun-scalded face heat as he focused his eyes straight on Stafford, who by now seemed aware of his strength.

"I have to tell you something." There. Got it out. If only I can keep going.

"Well, yes, part of my job, listening. What is it, Brother Fall?" Wardley leaned forward as if intensely interested, but his hands fidgeted with the paperweight with the snowflakes floating around the English Setter in the glass globe.

Brandon then knew that Stafford was attempting to be solicitous and unctuous to keep down his animosity.

"Now, Brother Stafford, I know White Oak Church folks had trust and faith in me." Amazing how his heart stopped knocking, and a real energy came right up to his tongue. Brandon shifted one lean leg over the other, foot encased in his work shoes, as the bottoms had fallen out of his Sunday ones.

"Why, yes. Why, yes, Brother Fall–"

"I responded to the White Oak folks' love and their call. I knew the Lord was with me. There was a future for me in the White Oak Church." Brandon's voice steadied now that he'd lifted the lid. He realized God gave him the strength.

"Well, Brother Fall, the Lord's ways are not always so clearly discerned, wouldn't want any young Christian to be overconfident."

"Brother Stafford, I have to tell you that you remind me of Balaam riding on that ass."

Bishop Stafford shifted his athletic body, his massive chest heaved, beads of sweat crept to his neck and slid down into the hair mat at his open collar. His eyes widened as if he thought, What nerve. Balaam?

Stafford seemed to realize he couldn't let the time drag, he had to gain the momentum. He cleared his throat. "Now, young man, I'm afraid I don't see the connection. You accusing me...." Stafford's cheeks turned burgundy.

"The connection? Brother Stafford, Balaam's ass was able to see and understand the will of the Lord better than Balaam himself. Don't you think it could be that you galloped right on in White Oak Church on your own donkey and may have ridden over the will of the Lord?" The silence hung between them.

Brandon's heart started pounding again, but at the same time he thought: God is giving me strength. I can't believe those words leaped out.

Wardley Stafford's square-shouldered body sagged in his chair. He raked his hand through his shock of hair, half-turning as if he'd suddenly lost his way. "Why, uh – you listen here, you young–"

"You lost Lissa over it, Brother Stafford. I'm glad. Lissa saw through you. So do I. It took a month. Yes. Balaam's ass saw what the prophet, himself, couldn't see – the angel of the Lord standing in the path. When Balaam disregarded his faithful donkey's turning aside, he was brought up short. Got his foot smashed against the wall; nearly got killed. Numbers 22."

"How did I let this happen? Opening my door to a wild-haired hillbilly prophet, next thing you know–" Stafford lurched to his feet.

"Well, Brother Stafford, I'm here to tell you whatever it was behind your cutting me loose, and I know Rhutley was in on it with you, I see through it." Brandon had both worn brogues flat on the floor. He leaned forward. A great peace suddenly swept through his soul.

"Why, uh, why, Brother Brandon, I ... I–"

"Brother Stafford, I want to tell you right now that I forgive you. I came here with a big ball of ill-will in my gut. God took it away, just like he took away Baalam's anger and refusal to open his eyes. I forgive you, Brother Stafford." He rose, looking down at the shaken man, discombobulated, hand fumbling for his glasses and knocking the massive concordance to the floor.

"Why, uh, Brandon, there's really nothing to for...." But it seemed to Brandon that guilt plastered Stafford's tongue against the roof of his mouth like old Baalam's foot smashed by the donkey against the wall. He could no longer speak.

"I can let myself out. Good-bye, Brother Stafford."

* * *

Five minutes passed before Wardley Stafford could raise his head from arms folded across the desk. He lifted both hands, raking his still trembling fingers through his hair. "Oh, God. Oh, God. Will there ever be any peace?" he mumbled. In spite of the ninety-five-degree heat, he shook with a chill.

* * *

As Brandon guided his chugging Model A down Main Street in Reeds Spring, then took a left turn toward the black-top towards Branson, he hung his left elbow out the window. Drought. Hard times. But how clean I feel inside, like a fresh shower. Lissa. Lissa's love. The future. Something greater than either of us calls. His thoughts were sweet as spring wind.

* * *

On the opposite side of town, a freshly polished burgundy Buick made a right turn onto Main Street in Reeds Spring, heading for the parsonage beside the brick church.

Marla Edith beamed in satisfaction with the new page-boy hairdo Cicily Woodburn had given her. A gold bracelet slid down near her hand, nails freshly painted in pink.

Surely glad Clementine got in that new line. This black pongee the proper dress for one who's about to call on the head of the conference, *Wardley Stafford*. Are the seams of my black-toned silk hose straight over my calves?

Glad too Clementine had these patent pumps to go with the dress, but I gotta watch it on four-inch heels. Marla Edith grinned, remembering Wyman Turney's comment on who knew how to walk in high heels.

Yes. Churchman Stafford lonely over here. I do believe that faithless Lissa who dumped a man like Wardley told him I stepped in the door and inquired about his health the day he made that announcement about hillbilly Brandon.

She turned the Buick into the driveway by the parsonage. She had enough money to take them both out for steak dinner tonight over at Sammy Lane Resort, if he was too caught up in the Lord's work to think of it.

Suddenly, the pain of her years of living out on that farm with her nearly silent mother, cowed by old Sloan, and trying to block out the endless criticisms and insults bandied about by folks against her pa, plus her desperate loneliness, lifted as hope seeped into the vacuum.

CHAPTER TWENTY-FIVE

Aunt Gustie didn't mind rattling along toward town with a used car salesman, so long as he didn't try to pawn off one of his pieces of junk on her. She yanked down the brim of her faded yellow straw hat and plonked herself on the right side of Melvin Pempton's Ford pickup. Assured of her conversation skills, she grinned in certainty that she'd be able to dig important information out of sweaty Melvin, while enduring the jolts to her ribs.

"The Maggler place? Sure, I'm driving by the Maggler place." Melvin twisted the toothpick in his mouth with his tongue and grinned.

The truck lumbered over a sagging bridge and plowed under the limbs of a dead cottonwood. A flock of buzzards, gathered around carrion in the road ahead, stared, flapped their wings, hissed, and staggered out of the way. The rear of the pickup whipped dangerously on the loose gravel. Gustie clutched the brim of her hat, her bones rattling.

She eyed the white frame Maggler house and the long walk up to the front porch and cleared her dry throat. "Thank ye mightily, Melvin. Oughta be easy to hop a ride back home, busy gravel road like this past the Magglers'." But Gustie had already concluded she would walk the four miles home if she had to.

She poked her old cracked-leather purse under her arm, the one her sister, Magdalene out in Tulsa, gave her back in 1903. She looked down at her high-topped shoes and gingham skirt, flaring out in the wind. "Well, here goes. I only had one other serious talk with a Maggler, and that was the time old Maggler foreclosed on the Hodge sisters' farm. Betcha old Sloan's hide still burns from the scalding I give him."

Marla Edith's little long-haired spaniel nipped at her heels and growled to announce her presence. Gustie lifted her sun-splotched hand to rap at the door, then jerked on the brim of her hat once more.

The door opened. "Why, why, uh – uh, Gustie, isn't it? They call you *Aunt* Gustie, don't they?" Marla Edith leaned out, her eyes bulging, round as cup-bottoms.

"That's who you're speaking to, Marla Edith. Spose I might say *Miss* Marla Edith, being's you're a schoolmom." Gustie reached out to hold back the screen door while at the same time leaning in as if she was determined to get into the shed ahead of a headstrong cow.

"Why, er, Gustie, or, Aunt Gustie, yes, come on in." Gustie was smart enough to know that Marla Edith would worry over what an old biddie like herself wanted and probably considered her no match for an experienced teacher like herself. Then, too, Marla Edith would want to hightail it over to Wardley Stafford and blab to him about this old hen barging in and ruining her morning.

Gustie was surprised that Marla Edith actually pointed out the blue wing chair near the bay window in the living room. Well, them Magglers do keep the dust wiped up from their stand tables, don't they? Gustie's river-gravel eyes surveyed the spacious room, drapes half-drawn to keep out the scalding sun.

Marla Edith drew up a little oak chair with roses carved in the back, needlepoint-covered seat.

Her calves sagged outwards when she crossed her legs. Gustie figured Marla Edith hated it she'd caught her in loafers and anklets. Would want to whisk her out soon. Gustie was sure of that.

"Something I'm a gonna go over with you, Marla Edith." Gustie's crooked index finger wagged in a sunbeam from the east window.

Marla Edith's big eyes opened with her most innocent look as if Gustie's visit had nothing at all to do with Lissa, or that sinew-and-bones Brandon, who was left dangling from that preaching job.

Gustie brought her cracked leather purse to her lap, fingers on the corroded clasp. "Now, I ain't a gonna sit here waitin around like a sick kitten on a jamrock." Gustie noticed Marla Edith's eyes turn beady as a water moccasin's. *It's a good thing I got a little livin under my belt.* She cleared her throat.

"My, what a way to express what you're getting at, Mrs., er, Aunt Gustie. That's what they call you?"

Gustie clawed in her purse and dragged out a stack of tied-up greenbacks, and one of those little tobacco sacks with the yellow drawstring, heavy with coins.

Marla Edith's mouth opened. "Why, yes. Get right down to business. Just what kind of business is it, Aunt Gustie?" Her eyebrows lowered as her face shifted into her Sunday School teacher look.

"Miss Marla, there's that matter of the forty dollars. Bible school money, I believe. The Lord's money. Yep – Bible school money."

Gustie cleared her throat again. She decided she'd better slow down so that her words could settle in like pork rinds tossed into the boiling lye water on soap-makin day.

"Forty dollars?" Marla Edith's query, innocent as an infant searching for a sugar tit. Her shoulder twitched at the rock-hard old woman's power. "Well, what of it? The Bible school money?" Marla Edith waited, shifting one catfish-belly calf.

"Well, I happened to know you took on the responsibility, before witnesses in the church, too, to send that money off right away to your Maggler cousin in Africa." Gustie's stare burned toward Marla Edith.

"Well, I, I. Yes, I, er...." Marla Edith choked.

"Never got it done, did you, Miss Maggler? Nope. I happen to know you compromised my neighbor, a young man of my own heart, Brandon Fall. I'm wonderin' if you ever meant to send it. You bowed and scraped, offering him what you *said* was the money you supposed to of sent on beforehand. You musta put that Bible School money in your own bank account."

Marla Edith shifted her legs as if she realized she'd have been more in control if she didn't have on her loafers and the ankle socks, nevertheless....

"That right, Marla Edith?" Gustie leaned in like a blacksnake hypnotizing a Buff Orpington hen on the nest.

"Well, I, er, I mean to still get the money sent, soon as that farmer Bran—"

"And, don't *'soon's'* me, Marla Edith Maggler. Your 'soon's' already ran out."

"What you want me to do, Gustie? Isn't it kind of late to be — Besides, Brandon Fall owes me the money. He was foolish enough to use my money as a down payment on that tinny Ford. You'd have thought he'd known better. Blame anybody, blame him." Marla shifted one heavy thigh over the other, betraying her fear of losing control.

"And don't talk about being late, Marla Edith. I bumped and jostled over here with *Melvin Pempton*. I believe you understand he knows just how long you stayed that Saturday night in that dance hall, you a schoolmom too, and how you cavorted out on that floor." Gustie's hand clawed at her shriveled throat, letting her words sink in — certain that Marla Edith was quite aware of what Melvin Pempton *knew* about her.

"Ask your old school board member, Silas Whitsitt, the one fired you, how you knocked your knees and swung them beads when you was out on the floor with Melvin doing the Charleston whilst everyone clapped and hooted. Want me to tell about it in Sunday School over at White Oak? Reverend Stafford'd want to know about it, wouldn't he?"

"Stop it." Marla Edith boiled. "Old hen like you come waddling into my living room. You threatening me, Gustie Simpson?"

"I'll stop when I please. Now. My mind recollects, too, you left the dance hall with Melvin and drove on over to Ozark to the Red Cock Roadhouse and didn't get back till nigh onto three in the morning."

Gustie knew that shifty Marla Edith was aware that when they have the goods on you, smile, agree, lean in, compromise a teeny.

"Agreement was Brandon would have to send it in. I loaned the money back to him. His responsibility. You can't hang that on me." Marla Edith's tongue stretched out to moisten the edges of her heavy lips.

"You ain't the one to be saying who's responsible. You're responsible, Marla Edith. You know Brandon and everyone else's corn didn't make this fall. He's working for fifty cents a day. Never make forty dollars."

"That's Brandon's problem. Oughtn't to be such a poor businessman."

"I know, too, Miss Maggler, you done a low-down, yellow-bellied thing. You sneaked off to the deacons of White Oak Church, sniveling and putting on like you'd been done in, when all the time it was you who held out on that money."

Gustie straightened her shoulders and reached for her straw hat, gaining more confidence.

"Now, now, Mrs. Gustie–"

"I got forty dollars. My store teeth money. Now, Marla Edith Maggler, you git that address out right now, that African Mission address. I want to lay my Arkansas-born eyes on it."

Marla Edith, who seemed in Gustie's eyes to unravel more than she had expected, rose and padded in her loafers to the secretary. She yanked open the bottom drawer. She closed it, yanked open another one. She stood on the sides of her shoes, digging and searching.

"And don't tell me you can't find it, cause I'm a not a'gonna leave until–"

"Here it is, Aunt Gustie, here it is." Marla Edith plopped on the edge of her chair. "You going to send that cash on in? Postmaster'll never send cash."

"No. *You* send a money order before the post office closes this very day, Marla Edith. Battery ain't dead in that Buick out yonder, is it? Take the forty dollars." Gustie dropped her teeth money in Marla Edith's lap. Her green skirt bagged under the weight of the coins.

"Well, I never, I can't have an old woman come in to my house and command me to...." Marla Edith railed. Her face leaked red through the olive tones. Her eyes black as water moccasin eyes.

"And another thing, on your way back, Marla Edith, you gonna stop at Deacon Silas Whitsitt's place and get out and hurry in and tell him with your own tongue that you sent the money like you first said you'd do. Tell 'em, too, that the deacons better call the church dogs off of Brandon Fall, cause if they don't, I'm a gonna tell them how you done. You're the one have to make a confession. More than one confession. That Charleston dance ain't *all* Melvin Pempton told me about on the way over here."

By now Gustie saw that Marla Edith had tremors in both legs. "I'll get my hat and start up the Buick right now, Gustie, I'll...."

"And," Gustie said, rising and limping for the door. "If I ever *hear* a word about that Bible School money again, I'm a gonna go personally and tell that Wardley Stafford, believe you know him. If it'd please you to know it, he gave me a right nice compliment one day when he took Sunday dinner at our house." Gustie couldn't help patting the wisp of hair dislodged in back.

Gustie left Marla Edith's house poorer than when she went in, but what did the Bible say about the poor? Anyway, she felt free as a schoolgirl just finished saying her recitation, putting Marla Edith Maggler in her place. Only thing, old Gustie hated it that she'd forgotten to add, as she headed down the walk, "You and Wardley Stafford surely do deserve each other."

CHAPTER TWENTY-SIX

Estra Massey stood by the staircase and watched as Slade grabbed another year's Christmas tree and dragged it through the door and on out to the the wood pile. Cedar all dried up, though she did love the smell of cedar. Now she could stretch out her dining room table.

Her high cheekbones flushed pink at the joy of having her brood around her Sunday table. Glad, too, the canned beef held out. "Always makes the best gravy, and I never knew a man who didn't like savory beef chunks on his plate," she had murmured to herself while stirring the brown gravy.

Estra's heart warmed at the sight of Lissa in her pale blue woolen dress with the long sleeves and pleated skirt sitting beside her fiancé, Brandon, in his best starched Sunday shirt and garter snake galluses. She figured he'd get a suit come April when they married. Important thing was, she decided, how that Brandon had gained a pound or two and some of the weariness had lifted from his shoulders, but of course, they all wondered: When would he hear from that seminary in Kansas City?

Aunt Gustie gummed her portion of beef. Next she sopped a chunk of Estra's light bread into the gravy and buried her face in it.

"Well, guess we can talk about it, Marla Edith and that starched-shirt Wardley Stafford, being's after services, Slade rode on over to the Hersheys in their Whippet to play with their boy, Raulsten." Gustie lifted her gravely eyes, a half-smirk on her mouth.

"I never thought Marla Edith would resign in the middle of the year. I haven't said much, on account of Slade, of course, but he likes the new teacher, Mr. Hyatt, much better, says he's able to teach algebra so he understands it." Lissa sipped from the green cornflower depression glass tumbler.

"And Lissa, getting your scholars all prepped for the county activity day won't be nearly so much fun without Marla Edith, will it?" Brandon grinned, bringing to their minds the tug of war between Lissa's and Marla Edith's schools last year.

"It's okay, Brandon. I don't need to exhaust myself like I did last year. We'll try hard. I know my students will do their best." Lissa thought of Tippy Mae, out of school now for half a year, her dad not even bothering to encourage her to go to high school.

"Well, now with Marla Edith settling in with the churchman Stafford, she won't need her school check, and it's a blessing that at least one more out-of-work man found a job, even at those wages." Estra had a point, all the starving-faced young men leaving for the WPA and the CCC.

"I never seen such a wedding in my life, and I've seen a few in my time, too," Gustie said.

"I only knew one other wedding held on Christmas Eve," Brandon added as he reached for another slice of Estra's bread.

"And Marla Edith insisting on having it at White Oak Church, said she wanted the charm of a country church, and she a member of that white-spired Branson church." Since the deacons agreed on the matter, Estra guessed she had no cause to complain.

"Tell you what I think about it. Only a bank loan officer like old Sloan Maggler could afford poinsettias. An' that spiffed-up Wardley Stafford standin' up there amongst them red leaves, watching Marla Edith swing down that aisle in a red dress and red high heels. Reminded me of somethin' in the book of Revelation." Gustie grumbled, pushing herself back a few inches from the table.

"What are you referring to, Aunt Gustie?" Brandon asked.

"Well, first off, I was sitting between Elda Holesopple and Beulah Hodge, rest of you didn't have *nerve* enough to go to the wedding." Gustie lifted her chin as if admiring her own strength to endure what many thought was about as tough a task as climbing Mt. Nebo in Arkansas on the hottest day of summer.

"Anyway, Elda leaned over and said, 'Red, why, ain't it a proper color for a wedding on Christmas Eve?'"

"I'd never choose it," Lissa said, her eyebrows raised.

"Well, being's Slade's not here, I'm a gonna tell you what Beulah Hodge said when she seen Marla Edith hip-walkin' down that aisle in her red dress. 'Why, if I'd a been dumped from my school like Marla Edith was, you think I'd have the gumption to dress up and parade down the church aisle in red? Red? Color that bad woman they tell about in the book of Revelation wore, ain't it?' Beulah's eyes nearly stayed crossed from rolling them like she done." Gustie's own eyes bugged out, her lips half-circled down.

Estra's fork clanked on the edge of her plate. Lissa's cheeks blushed, and her mouth closed tightly as she stared at her potatoes and gravy. Brandon grinned.

"Gustie, Gustie, we must be charitable, and I believe the color your friend referred to in the Bible was *purple*. I'm sure Marla Edith regrets some of her past behaviors, but don't we all? Let's not pass judgment or cast slurs. Too much pain in the world for that."

Though chided, Gustie continued. "Well, that new preacher, Elwin Nevins, young as he was, handled it about like he'd finished teaching a calf to suck from a bucket. He only stuttered once, marrying a chief Elder, but anyone else would have swallered their tongue."

"Well, let's all hope it lasts, Brother Wardley and Marla Edith. We should pray for them. We all know how lonely he was." Then Brandon slid his arm down and clasped Lissa's warm hand.

"You two might as well take a drive over to Branson and look at that rental house listed in *The Gazette*. Might want to put something down to hold it. April'll be here before you know it." Estra's smile reflected her hope, wedding in April, fine new son-in-law. Both of them, Lissa and Brandon, faith challenged, but faith intact.

"We'll do that, Estra, and this evening my mother wants us to stop by after services. She made two pies out of those Jonathans you gave her."

* * *

Brandon and Lissa agreed that they should not go ahead and put up the rent three months in advance for the four-room house in Branson.

"No, much as I'd like to, Lissa, it'd be a waste of money. Way folks are moving around the country these days, surely there'll be something else if this house isn't available when we marry."

Lissa stared at the small white frame house on Lynn Street, overshadowed by a black walnut on each side. Yard small, brown in winter, gravel driveway leading up to the side by the spreading tree. "Brandon, no trumpet vine. We'll have to order a trumpet vine from Henry Field's, won't we?" She brushed back a blond wisp of hair as they sat in the green Model A in front of the house.

The February sun beaming through the windshield and windows of the car warmed the interior. Lissa unbuttoned the top button of her blue wool coat with the silvery opossum shawl collar.

Brandon reached for her hand and noticed how warm it felt, small too – the strength behind it. The goodness, the love. His bright eyes and the pulse throb at his neck announced the joy Lissa Massey brought to his heart. "April, Lissa? We have to wait until April?"

"Yes, my love. When school's over. It's better that way." She pressed his callused hand.

The house beckoned them, its friendly windows and tiny porch with the two posts seeming to say, "Come and sit a while."

Each felt the other's calm faith, even though they were living through the nation's most poverty-stricken years. Folks leaving by droves for Texas or California. Relief truck parking down by the railroad station every other week, passing out government surplus: cheese, potatoes, canned goods, cereal. Everybody wearing runover shoes. Younger children in most families thankful for hand-me-downs. The town sagged with the weight of the times. Dust and leaves swirled in doorways of closed stores. It would be only a matter of time before the depot would close, as well as the bank. Could the grocery store endure?

Their young hearts beat in faith – the faith that gives courage for one day at a time. Hope that allows one to see the tomorrows' horizons as a welcoming glow.

They had discussed moving in with Lissa's family, or with Owney and Serena, though Brandon knew they would have to add on a room if they chose the latter. "Ours is such an old ramshackle-of-a-house, anyway, Lissa...." Brandon hung his head.

"You'll see, Brandon. Doors will open. Remember, when I couldn't find a school two summers ago, how Silas Whitsitt drove down and practically forced me to sign up for Blue Vale?"

"Yes, Lissa." A gnawing at his gut reminded him that it hadn't worked that way for him. What seemed like an opportunity at White Oak Church, the planned ordination, scattered by the winds of deceit and betrayal. Then it came to him: God also works through such painful events, deceit, betrayal. Positions jerked out from under you. Could it be? Could events such as these cause a surge of faith?

Brandon started the Ford, put it in low, and headed slowly down Lynn Street toward Main. "Let's take a circle around the neighborhood and out by Table Rock, Lissa, south into those hills, fine day like this."

Lissa relaxed, allowing herself the luxury of an easy afternoon with the man who loved her. When they approached the little stone bridge over Sugar Creek, Brandon pulled to the side beneath the white-barked sycamore. "Let's get out, soak up some of this sun while we watch what water there is trickle through the rocks."

They leaned over the bridge rail. Brandon tried not to allow the almost dry stream to depress him. A sudden wind shook the giant sycamore limbs above.

A small flock of Canada geese who hadn't made it all the way to the Gulf of Mexico rose from Dillon's pond, circled, honked, and dipped eastward towards White River.

"Better go. Services at White Oak at seven tonight. After church, Mother expects your family, Lissa. Aunt Gustie too. She's a real prize." Brandon placed his arm around Lissa's waist as they strolled back to the Model A.

"Aunt Gustie is dear and special. Yes, she's a prize." Lissa smiled, remembering her aunt's vow to attend services more regularly. "I didn't realize how much gumption she had, hitch-hiking with Melvin Pempton that day all the way over to Magglers."

"She surely rattled Marla Edith's bones, dumping her teeth money in her lap, insisting she send it and clear things up with the deacons," Brandon grinned.

"I know it worries you, Brandon, not able to pay Aunt Gustie back yet."

So far he'd paid nine dollars, but he could scarcely save more out of fifty cents a day, not being able to work every day of the week either.

They both realized the days called for faith.

CHAPTER TWENTY-SEVEN

Lissa looked over her schoolroom at the thirteen scholars. All year long she had missed Tippy Mae's bulk in the back desk where she dominated the row last year. She decided to drive by Tippy Mae's house to see if she could offer to tutor her in math so she could get into high school next year.

Needa Hodge took the lead in this year's activity day play. They'd placed second, but Needa hadn't brought down the house like Tippy Mae did last year.

Orbert and Elroy Terfer helped their team win the relay. Louis and Lottie Wincet had matured enough to stop most of their quarreling at lunch time.

Lissa thought of her wedding coming up in two weeks. Already, she and Brandon had met with new Pastor Nevins in the five-room house adjoining the church. Elwin had sat in his study, listening to their plans, smiling, willing to comply. Mentioned he thought he'd select a passage from the Song of Solomon. "What hymns do you want, Lissa? It ought to be you who makes the selection."

"Why, Brandon and I both want *O Perfect Love*, Pastor Nevins. Can you see to it that Ida Lou can play the organ for us?"

Lissa had decided that if there were any April rains at all, they'd have roses, everblooming Red Scarlets, and pink and yellow Talismans. Also, for filler in the bouquets, there would be forsythia, if an early killing frost didn't ruin it like two years ago. April? There would be jonquils and iris, too, and don't forget the lilacs.

Her dress? Yes, Lissa had given thought to her dress.

"Mother, I really don't want to take precious money and spend it at Clementine's for one of her bridal dresses and veil. They run as much as thirty-nine dollars. I can open up the Singer and sew up a little white suit that would match a white hat I could order out of Sears."

"Well, yes, you could. Of course, I'd help you sew it. But let's take a look at my wedding dress."

Estra's eyes glowed with a light Lissa hadn't seen for months as she turned for the stairwell and headed for the armoire in the east bedroom upstairs. When she returned, she held the folds of drooping silk in her arms.

"Mother, I'd forgotten it was so lovely."

Estra lifted the garment by the front shoulders, draping it before her body. "Yes, it was and still is a fine gown, Lissa. Jessee always said it was a perfect dress for me."

Lissa reached for the dress, noting that it would fit her, as her mother was her size at her age.

"It hasn't yellowed at all, Mother, has it?"

"No. Kept it wrapped in white tissue paper and in the big armoire drawer. A good silk. Aunt Dora and I ordered the pattern from the Simplicity book under their wedding gown section."

Estra, head shaking slightly, smiled as if she was recalling her wedding in the little church by the river in Branson in June 1910.

"Quite a chore, figuring out the ins-and-outs of that pattern. But once Aunt Dora understood it, she sewed on it until she finished. Seven yards of silk. She always loved the way the sleeves turned out, those Calla lily points, and the covered buttons on the bodice."

Lissa noticed tears in her mother's eyes, yet a smile of deep happiness.

"If you would like to wear it, Lissa, I'd be so—"

"Oh, Mother, yes. Yes. A perfect solution. I'll go upstairs and slip it on. Come on up with me."

Lissa's eyes gleamed as she glanced at herself in the bureau mirror. The pleated skirt was a little long, but Estra, good seamstress that she was, would even that out in no time at all.

"I believe we could buy a little netting, Lissa, and make you a veil that would add more charm to the dress and wouldn't cost much at all."

"I'd like it, Mother. Oh, I do know Brandon will be surprised when he sees me coming down the aisle in such a lovely dress. And Mother, look at the money we'll save."

* * *

Lissa closed the schoolroom window as a breeze whipped through, rattling papers on her desk. She glanced up at the great billowing clouds crowning Inspiration Point. She thought of Brandon, glad he'd been able to save enough money to march into Hoover's Men's Wear and pick out a new navy suit, one he hoped would last years beyond the wedding date. Surprised that he could get such a good suit for nineteen dollars, Brandon planned to buy new dress shoes the Saturday before the wedding.

The schoolroom clock ticked. The scholars studied geography and arithmetic during the study hour. Outside, the April wind whipped at the schoolhouse eaves. Lissa couldn't help but think of her hope chest in the hall upstairs by her bedroom door.

White chenille bedspread, three gorgeous hand-stitched quilts, the dazzling Tulip-Tree-patterned one made by the White Oak Church sewing circle. Dishes. Ladies of the church having a shower for me next Friday after school. Wonder if they remember I only wanted the Cabbage Rose depression glass that comes in the oatmeal and cereal boxes? Don't want to be a burden to anyone.

Towels? Washcloths? Aunt Gustie had embroidered seven Sunbonnet Girls tea towels with differing colors and outlines.

Brandon promised to help Slade turn the crank on the ice cream freezer the day of the bridal shower. After the ice cream was frozen, he promised to take Slade to a ball game in the park by White River. "A man has to get out of the way of his sweetheart's bridal shower, Lissa," he said.

When the arithmetic and geography lessons were over, Lissa excused the scholars. Four o'clock. It didn't take long to grab the broom and sweep the oiled plank floor. And this late in the spring, she needed only to take one coal bucket out to the shed for lumps of coal. Maybe wouldn't even need to fire up the big potbellied stove next morning, sun keep warming the days like today.

Lissa brushed the dirty sawdust into her dust pan, emptied it, and straightened the desks evenly in their rows. Next she washed the blackboard, then dusted the erasers on the back of the schoolhouse. She grabbed her scarf and jacket and headed for her mother's Model A.

I wonder how Marla Edith and Brother Stafford are doing? I doubt that Marla Edith will be satisfied with that house in Branson. She'll insist on having Reverend Stafford at least move her up to Springfield. Wonder it hasn't happened by now. Lissa's foot hit the starter.

Is it true, Marla Edith and Wardley Stafford hiring Tippy Mae to be chore girl at their place? Lissa decided to find out. She plowed out of the schoolyard lane.

CHAPTER TWENTY-EIGHT

The next Monday, April rain, swept by westerly winds, poured over Inspiration Point and down into the valley. The thirsty land soaked the cool droplets. The sounds of gurgling streams were heavenly in folks' ears.

"My, we'll have lilacs after all. And look at the forsythia bush, Brandon," Serena said, out on the front porch to take stock of the spring greening.

"Brings one hope, doesn't it, Mother, after the last two years. I'm going to head out to the pasture, believe Molly had her calf earlier today. See if she's all right and bring the new calf in."

Brandon stepped along the rain-softened gravel path, heart rejoicing at the bright green leaves popping through on the dogbane, the gooseberry bushes, and the buckeye. White clouds towered against the deep blue sky.

He wore his old leather boots to keep his pant legs dry as he tromped deeper into the brush alongside the woods. He began to hum a verse from the song Lissa'd selected for their wedding, last Sunday in April.

> O perfect Love, all human thought transcending,
> Lowly we kneel in prayer before thy throne,
> That theirs may be the love which knows no ending,
> Whom Thou forevermore dost join in one.

He thanked God for bringing about Lissa's and his love. A vision of Lissa in the church, wearing a dress she'd hinted of, surfaced in his mind. He couldn't help smiling.

Brandon halted to listen for lowing or rustling of cow or calf. Hearing neither, he continued a few rods more on the crooked path which led into the undergrowth by Dodie Creek. Already the sweet william's heady aroma swept over the path, lined with the bright green sour dock and new poke.

Whew. Hot. April day steamy. Bring out the living creatures for sure. Brandon swatted at a bottle fly zinging his neck. Then he removed his old felt hat to run his fingers through his hair.

The wind, months ago, had blown down an old rotting maple alongside the path, the biggest limb having fallen directly over the path where Brandon tromped.

Buried in his thoughts about the wedding and how glad both Serena and Estra would be at the flowers following these showers, he forgot Owney's advice to him as a child. "Never step across a fallen log in the pathway. Instead, step up on a limb, or log, look, then plant your foot on the other side."

Brandon's fine long leg reared up astraddle the moss-etched log, weight of his body tilting forward. His booted right leg followed as he continued his easy swing, eyes focusing in the undergrowth at the pathsides for old Molly and her calf. "No Molly," he murmured, catching his balance and keeping his stride.

"Ouch," he muttered, glancing back at what he believed to be the gooseberry branch that'd caught his left leg just above the top of his leather boots. "Those gooseberry thorns dig and scratch," he mumbled.

"Molly! Molly! Soooooo cow. Sooooo cow," he called. Brandon reached down to rub his leg where the thorn had pierced his pant leg, but he felt no lodged thorn and kept up his stride.

By the time he rounded another bend, Dodie Creek footbridge just ahead, he decided he'd better stop, rest a moment on the old elm stump surrounded by the dogtooth violets and take a look at where the thorn had scratched him. "Whew, it's hot – real pain streaking through my left leg." Suddenly his head swirled, and his legs bent and wobbled. Sweat beaded his forehead. *Was I walking that fast?*

He stopped to check his left leg above the boot top. No tear, only wetness, but then the weeds and brush were heavy with water. Yet, his breathing slowed and became shallow. The lightheadedness increased with a pulsing burn just above his knee.

Brandon decided he'd better untie the boot and check. He realized an insect bite could be nasty. Hadn't stalked through any nettles, had he?

The boot dropped, Brandon lowered his stocking, but the trouble was above his knee. A bruise? What is it? Leaning closer and squinting, Brandon saw the two punctures, as if someone had pierced his thigh with a two-pronged fork. Beads of blood oozed.

No. Can't be. Not snakebite? Didn't hear any rattling. Not a rattler. Copperhead? Well, yes. Day hot enough to bring out a copperhead, early as it is. Even known them to creep out on a rock in late March.

Then the searing pain hit full force. Scarlet flashed before his eyes. He gasped for breath. Snakebite. No. No. And our wedding....

The nasty wound swelled, turning purple, the little pierced flesh points closing.

"Oh, Lord above. Gotta get my knife open right here."

Brandon reached for his penknife. His left hand dug for his red handkerchief.

"Gotta twist it and get it around my thigh about four inches above the bite. How can I do it with such piercing pain? Dear God, don't let me pass out."

For a moment he saw Lissa before his eyes, her face, her smile as if she were gathering lilacs in her yard.

"Not too tight. Cut off the blood completely, bring on gangrene."

He inserted his index finger beneath the constricting band he'd made from his red handkerchief. "It ought to do."

"Oh, dear Lord above, help me."

Next, in spite of his shallow breathing and the drenching sweat, his hand was still steady as he opened the big razor-sharp blade of the knife.

"Here goes. Lord, here goes."

Brandon knew that he'd have to make two X-es into the skin and flesh on each side of both fang marks. Blood flowed along with greenish-looking venom.

"Oh, God, help me." Brandon wondered if he was going to fall off the stump, so he lowered himself to the path below. Then, steadying himself and catching his breath, he made the incisions alongside the other fang mark.

"How did Uncle Vilus do it the time the rattler struck him? Suck at the cut, spit it out. Suck at it."

Brandon leaned over, praying that he wouldn't pass out. He drew at the wounds. He spat. He drew, lips against the purple flesh and oozing blood. He spat. His stomach wrenched and roiled.

"Have to get home. Have to drag home."

Picking up a broken limb from the old elm, he heaved to his feet while holding the boot in his left hand. By now it seemed as if the spring sweetness, the billowing clouds against the blue sky, the fragrance of violets, the shiny tops of the sprouting mayapples, all were mingling into one blooming confusing, whirling around him as a great buzzing zinged in his eardrums.

* * *

Serena put down her sewing and ambled out the screen door. "Owney, what's that dog carrying on so about?"

Then she saw a wobbling, bent-over figure, staggering, heaving himself up past the barn toward the house.

"Owney, it's Brandon. He's sick." Serena leaped off the porch, through the yard gate past the first of the purple irises and down toward the barn.

"Brandon, Brandon, what is it? Oh, my God."

Serena caught him as he tottered toward her. "Mother. Snake bite. Probably copperhead. Didn't see the snake."

God, help me get into the house. Can't pass out here. Mother couldn't get me into the house alone. Brandon was losing consciousness.

"Oh, my God. Son. What are we to do?" Serena half-dragged him as his full weight lay upon her. "You've got to make it, Brandon. Only a few more steps. Oh, Lord, help us."

Brandon, straining and groaning, made it up the three steps and into the house and into Serena and Owney's bedroom by the kitchen. He fell back, head and shoulders on the spread.

Serena reached down and lifted the purplish leg and his other booted foot to the bed. "Oh, Lord God. What shall I do? What shall I do?" She wrung her hands.

By now Owney had reached his crutch and had dragged himself into the small room, paralyzed arm swinging. "Oh, son. Snakebite? Yes, you've already made those incisions."

The ringing in Brandon's ears was by now a cataract of water pouring over his brain, his soul, washing through his sinew and muscle and bone, carrying him past boulders and giant black-trunked trees, away....

"Son, try to stay conscious. Serena, go get my razor. Gotta make two more incisions, bout four inches above where he's already cut. We'll see you through this, son."

Serena's hard heels hit the floor boards as she returned with the razor. "I can do it, Owney, you tell me where."

Serena steadied herself as Owney pointed, four inches above the green, oozing wounds. "There, Serena, there. Brandon, it's a gonna hurt like the dickens, but it'll save your life. Cut, Serena."

By now a goodly portion of the searing pain burning through Brandon's body also seared through both Serena and Owney's.

"Check the tourniquet, Serena. If he's got it on too tight, blood poisoning or gangrene might set in later."

Brandon passed out into blissful oblivion.

"Owney, I gotta go for help." Then Serena realized she hadn't learned to drive the new Model A – all those gears to shift. "Oh, Lord above. What am I going to do?" She turned, her face white with fear, eyes stark pools as she stared at Owney.

"You best get out on the road, Serena. Don't take time to round up a mule. Get yourself out on the road and head for Lit Watson's store. Telephone there. Neighbors shopping for groceries. Better than heading across Dodie Creek to Masseys. Three miles that way, though they do have a phone. Call for Doctor Sedgeley there in Branson. Take too long for an Ozark doctor to make it out here."

Serena realized she'd better get herself out on the road and keep herself visible. "Best chance that someone'll drive along, that way.

Yes," she replied.

While Owney sat by Brandon untying the right boot with his good hand, tussling to remove it, he held the callused hand of his beloved son. "Brandon, my boy. My boy, who always wanted to be a preacher." He prayed silently, lined face dripping tears. "Heal him, Lord. Lord, don't let him lose a leg."

CHAPTER TWENTY-NINE

Serena loped down the wet gravel road, spring frogs in the water-filled ditches shrieked, "Better run faster, better run faster."

Should have remembered to bring my purse. Oh, well, get to Lit's store, he'll call Doctor Sedgeley for me. Serena hobbled in an unbalanced gait, head bent over facing the track beneath her runover work shoes, her bent back throwing her weight off center.

Nevertheless, the heart-pained woman never broke stride, though her head roared with confusing thoughts and prayers: Oh, God, and he a getting married, too. Oh, Lord Jesus, how?

Behind Serena, an old canvas-topped coupe rounded the bend, front end shimmying. She turned and saw Amelia Longhorn aiming her car down the middle of the road. Amelia, probably on her way to Watson's store to sell her eggs and buy some sugar.

Amelia's car horn blasted. "A-oooooo-ga. A-ooooo-ga."

"Oh, blessed Amelia," Serena mumbled as she tottered to the edge of the road, her shoes sinking into mud. Amelia hit her brakes and the car halted in the soft gravel tracks. She stared out her splattered windshield at Serena Fall, no sweater, no smock, no hat, not even a purse.

Serena turned her pain-stricken face as Amelia leaned her head out the coupe window. "Why, Serena Fall. What you doing out on the road in this steamy heat without your hat?"

"Oh, thank the Lord, Amelia. Thank the Lord." Serena grasped for the door handle. "Take me on down the road, Amelia, to Lit's store. Oh, mercy, mercy. Amelia, Brandon's been snakebit bad." Serena buried her face in her work-gnarled hands.

Amelia's green eyes opened wide; "Was it a rattler, Serena? Lord, Lord...."

"Think it was a copperhead, Brandon didn't see the snake. Didn't hear any rattle. Terrible wound. Terrible wound. Amelia, hurry, hurry."

The old car shook and trembled, but Amelia kept it in the tracks as they rolled down the hill toward Dodie Creek. The closer they got, the more the creek's roar flooded their ears.

"Look at the ford, Serena." Amelia let up on the gas pedal and shoved in her brake as the rear end of the car scooted sideways in the wet sand.

"Why, Serena Fall, we're not going to be able to get across the ford until that water goes down." They leaned into the cracked windshield and stared at the boiling water; a broken branch with new green leaves swept past in the middle of Dodie Creek. Across, the lower limbs of the willows and maples bowed and dug in the roiling waters.

Serena prayed. "Oh, Lord Jesus, what am I going to do?" It was a cry of the poor, of the desperate. The mother's cry of love. "My son, my son."

"Water'll go down, Serena, but it'll take an hour or so, that is if it doesn't come up another rain. Big black cloud over west there." Amelia stretched to look westward.

Mercifully, a car swayed around the bend on the opposite shore of Dodie Creek. Pulling up to the descending grade, the old Chevrolet stopped, overall-clad man, gripping the wheel, disgusted look creasing his face.

"Why, Serena, isn't that Deacon Rennart?" Amelia hit her horn again. The grating unpleasantness of its blarings dislodged a flock of blackbirds who had settled in the sycamore by the roaring creek. They added their piercing cries to the water's roar as they soared and dipped over the creek.

"Yes, It's Rhutley. Thank the Lord." Serena leaped out the tinny door. "Mr. Rennart!" No time to be polite and ask, how are you this evening? "Mr. Rennart, my son Brandon's been bad snakebit. Big copperhead. Can you turn around and.... "

But Rennart had trouble understanding the bobbing old woman yelling at him. He flung open the door of his car, thumb under one of the galluses on his bib overalls and sauntered up to the edge of the flooding creek.

"Why, that you, Serena Fall? What you say? Mr. Fall doing poorly?"

"Rhutley, snakebite, snakebite." Serena yelled. "Brandon's been bitten by a copperhead. Can you turn around and hurry back to Lit Watson's store and call Doctor Sedgeley?" Can you, please?" Serena broke into tears, hiding her face in her hands.

By now Amelia had gotten out of the car, a sudden wind whipping the skirt of her violet calico around her heavy thighs. "Can you hear us, Mr. Rennart? Serena Fall, here, needs the doctor to come out to her place over on the ridge. We'd like to ask you to turn your car around and...."

By now Rennart understood the message.

"Oh, Lordy. You'all say snakebit? Copperhead? Oh, my, Mrs. Fall, why, when Filus Heavener got–" But he didn't finish. Besides they all knew that after only four days, they buried Filus in the Mt. Olive cemetery.

"I'll go. Doctor Sedgeley? Yes. I'll call him up. 'Spect he'll have to take the long way around, over the bridge by Four Crossing. Nine miles to your house that way, Serena, but if I can reach him, Sedgeley'll come."

Rhutley leaped into his Chevrolet, ground the starter, put it in reverse, and began to maneuver the turn. But his brakes were worn, and the road sloped toward the ditch, slick and steep. He grunted and strained, then shoved in the brake pedal. Too late, the back end of the rust-colored Chevrolet lurched and slid backwards into the three-foot-deep water-filled ditch.

Serena and Amelia could hear his mutterings as old Rennart got out, beating the back end of his car with his striped engineer's cap. They watched him throw up his arms as he began to hightail it up the road to Boad Bundy's farm for help.

Serena and Amelia clutched their hands in silence, hearts sinking, while the wind howled through the bending buckeye trees.

Rhutley turned back to holler, "I'll walk back to Bundy's, Serena. See if he can hook up the mule team and come back here." But his words were swept away by the wind and water's roar.

"Turn around, Amelia. Can't you turn around without getting in the ditch?" Serena's eyes pleaded.

"Well, I can try, Serena, where you want me to drive?"

"Drive back to where the woods ends and to the footbridge over Dodie Creek. Three miles back. A mile across the bridge to Lissa Massey's place. Oh, Amelia, we've got to tell Lissa."

They slammed the tinny doors. Amelia started her car, her eyes wide with fear. Her legs trembled. "Pray for me, Serena. Ain't easy turning around when the road is muddy and slick. Those grades on the sides, steep."

"Oh, blessed relief, Amelia, one more turn and you've made it. Yes." Sweat poured down Amelia's brow. Beads hung on the faint mustache on her upper lip.

The car chugged, backfiring twice. "Buford Turpinstep says I need a new timer, whatever that is, Serena, but we're gonna make it."

And they did. "I'm going to park here, Serena, by the buckeye and head through the brush with you. Not going to let you walk that mile alone and maybe the water's over the footbridge. Grab a stick."

"Yes. Stick. Snakes. Dear Lord." Serena bowed and hobbled down the muddy path toward the bridge, parting the bluebells with her feet, old hazel stick in her hand, eyes on the muddy path for the sight of a snake.

"Water's not over the footbridge yet, Amelia." Serena's breath caught, her chest heaved, the back of her dress plastered to her curved spine. They fanned their way through clouds of gnats and mosquitos.

"Look out, over there, old black snake longer'n you, Amelia, stretched out on that limb. Shinier than Abner Odom's patent leather shoes over at the funeral parlor."

"I see him, Serena. I see him." Amelia, heavier than Serena, heaved and panted.

Their feet crushed the new spring mushrooms popping through the wet soil and steam. "Ain't seen mushrooms like these couple of seasons, now," Amelia called out. "Too bad we can't take time to pick some of these an' fry 'em fer supper, Serena."

* * *

Lissa stepped out on the porch to see why Rufus was barking and carrying on so out by the gate. Serena? Amelia Longhorn loping up through the mud of the barnyard?

"Mother, step out on the porch, here come Brandon's mother and Amelia Longhorn plodding through the barnyard. What on earth?"

"Lissa. Lissa, oh, Lissa," Serena called, nearly fainting from the strain of her gallop in the mud, which, by now, had plastered the backs of her legs.

"Brandon's been bitten by a snake. Oh, Lissa...." Serena staggered, reached for the gate, and caught herself.

"Serena says it's bad, Lissa. We tried to drive to Watson's store to call Doctor Sedgeley, but water's too high at the ford." Amelia sank on the porch steps, her dress torn where she'd caught it in the wild rose bush on the path behind the barn.

Lissa, hand at her mouth, eyes staring, leaned forward, Estra's arm around her waist. "Do you know what kind of snake, Serena? Oh, dear Heavenly Father, reach down from your heaven and touch him, oh, God...."

"Think it was a copperhead. Brandon said he didn't hear a rattle, and he's got good ears. In the woods, looking for Molly and her new calf. Stepped over a log. Oh, Lissa, we cut his leg and tried to draw out the poison, but...." She bent her head and wept.

"Serena tried to get to the phone. Lissa, better try first to get Dr. Sedgeley. Maybe Rhutley Rennart made it to Watson's store and called already. Oh, Lissa, and you two about to be married."

Estra had already grabbed the phone. "Central? This you, Louise? Yes, Doctor Sedgeley, please. Yes."

The trio surrounded Estra, leaning in, shoes of two of them muddying the floor.

"Hello, Mrs. Sedgeley? This is Estra Massey nine miles out on the other side of the footbridge over Dodie Creek. I'm afraid I have to tell the doctor Brandon Fall's been bitten by a snake, a-a....

A BRANSON LOVE

What's that? Already knows about it? Well, that's a good thing. Then I'll tell Serena here, and Lissa that they ought to head on over to the Fall place on the ridge. Yes. Good bye." Estra hung the earpiece in its cradle on the side of the oak-encased phone.

"Thank the Lord. Rhutley Rennart ran in to Harley Soliver before he got the team to get his car out of the ditch. Harley hurried on back to the store and put in the call to Branson. Nine miles out to your place, Serena, coming by way of the bridge."

"Mother, I'll start up the Ford. Hurry, everyone, we've got to get back to Brandon. Oh, merciful Father...."

Slade stepped up on the porch, eyes reflecting confusion and fear at seeing the near-frenzied women. "What is it, Lissa?"

"Slade, Brandon's been bitten by a copperhead. We're driving on over. We'll depend on you to do the milking tonight." Lissa kissed her brother's cheek.

"I just remembered," Amelia said. "I left my coupe sitting on the side of the road by the woods leading to the footbridge. Mercy. Now what am I a gonna do?"

"You can ride with Mother, Serena, and me, Amelia. We'll get back to your car sometime tonight."

"I can't tromp through that woods path again, snakes coming out as they are in this heat. Oh, dear God."

"Slade," Estra said, "you and Rufus go with Amelia back across the footbridge to her car. Rufus'll warn you of any snakes."

"Yes. Yes, oh, thank you, Slade. We'd better go. Just think, I only started out to get five pounds of sugar, going to make some walnut pralines, and look where it led me. Oh, Lissa, Serena, I'm praying for Brandon, every step." Rufus, Slade, and Amelia headed through the yard gate, plodding through the mud on down through the Jimson weed and the barnyard.

The other three rode, Lissa gripping the wooden wheel as they headed eastward past Blue Vale School. The road circled and wound about the tree-covered hills. Any other time, all of them would have exclaimed: "Why, would you look at that plum thicket? Never saw blossoms so white." Or, "This is my favorite place, this vale here, bluegrass pasture yonder, and that line of cedars, and red bud. Did you ever see so much sweet william as this year?"

Instead, Estra, in the front seat, sat praying. She had remembered to grab the big Dutch oven on her stove filled with navy beans and ham hocks. It hunched between her shoes. "Bringing it along, Serena. You folks not going to take time tonight for cooking. I can stir up some cornbread when I get to your place."

They rode, all praying, all hoping, tears in their eyes. Lissa shifted into second gear as they approached Buzzard Hill. "Dear God in heaven, help us get there in time. Oh, Lord above, have mercy," she prayed as the tears streamed down her cheeks.

CHAPTER THIRTY

Lissa sat by the white-painted iron bed in the Ozark Hospital ward. Brandon's leg, swollen hip-sized from the thigh to his ankle; toes, bulbs like Christmas lights at the end of a football-sized foot. The purplish leg lay elevated on blanket rolls, partly gauze-covered, partly exposed.

"He's doing better today, Miss Massey, but he still isn't out of danger. Those pit viper bites take their toll on a body, destroy the red blood cells carrying oxygen and food to the muscles. Makes healing a real tussle."

Doctor Bowen poked his stethoscope into the pocket of his white coat. "You ought to take a lunch break, Miss Massey, you've been sitting here all morning."

"Thank you, Doctor, for your concern. I think I'll see if they can bring a sandwich here. I'd rather not leave him yet." Her blue eyes focused on Brandon's pale face, highlighted by his rich brown eyebrows and closed lashes.

"It's a blessing he can sleep now. The morphine will keep him comfortable for a while. I'll see him again on my evening rounds. I've asked Nurse Wills to give him as much special attention as she can."

The doctor gone, Nurse Wills, a short, stocky woman whose nursing cap peaked, then jutted backwards into two angular shafts on her red hair, smiled. "I've attended several who've made it through this, Miss Massey. You'll see. It's coming slowly. You'll see."

"Oh, dear God. Yes. Yes." Lissa reached up to touch the nurse's hand on her shoulder.

"It's the infection. Most of them get infection unless we get them in the hospital right away. Cutting with those knives out in the woods, or the razors at home. The lancing helped, yes. But usually leads to something like this."

A spring breeze blew through the half-opened window with the white organdy curtain, and drifts from the dogwood blossoms wafted into the hospital ward.

Oh, I wish we could have afforded a private room. Ward. Sixteen stark beds along a bleak wall. Mercy. Mercy. Oh, Lord Jesus. Lissa prayed.

Nurse Wills stepped away. Lissa glanced at the glass vase of six white and six red carnations amidst the contrasting fern leaves. A half-hour ago, aide Ellen Lutes had waddled in, holding the bouquet high in the air: "My, my, well, you'ns must be very important people. Says here on this card, 'From the Reverend and Mrs. Wardley E. Stafford.' My, my, real high-up folks."

Lissa looked out the window at the tops of the dogwoods and hoped it would calm the tumbling thoughts. Yes, the way life is – bitterness and forgiveness. Well, I have to let it go.... Grace of God takes it away. We are forgiven as we forgive.

In spite of her thoughts, Lissa recognized that there was still a part of her, left unchecked, that would have liked to have pitched the vase of flowers right out the open window.

Thoughts of Marla Edith swirled in her mind. She smiled, remembering little Ida Jane Ortis who'd yelled out, "Twist-up Oliver Tractor," and stopped Marla Edith's Oliver Rutley cold in his tracks, allowing her school to win the trophy. She thought of dear Tippy Mae. How was she? She wondered if Wardley Stafford and Marla Edith bore down on the gangling teenager with too much authority. "Fetch this, hurry, hurry, hurry." Lissa hoped not.

"You best take a break, little woman." The white-headed man with the weathered face attempted a smile from his bed behind Lissa.

Lissa drew back the thin curtain in order to reply. "I will, this afternoon, Mr...."

"Prouty. Seth Prouty from beyond Four Crossing."

Lissa didn't have to ask why he was in the hospital, his leg, elevated by a sling and in a cast, told the tale.

"Barn struck by lightning during that storm a week ago. Trying to get the milk cows out when a beam fell and caught my leg. Well, that time I was surely glad I married Matilda, she weighs nigh on to two hundred pounds, and without her, I'd a been a goner." Seth grinned across the gaps in his upper teeth.

"You can be thankful for a faithful wife, Mr. Prouty. Thankful."

Lissa's head lowered. We musn't worry about the medical bills. I have my last teaching check. Maybe Mother can help, or if they'd let us pay it on time payments. Poor Serena. Poor Owney. I must drive out and bring them in this evening. Last thing I want Brandon to hear when he comes to, is that his family had to go on relief.

Lissa thought of their wedding date, now past. When? June? "Oh, God, when?" She spoke the words to herself as she reached over to hold Brandon's hand. Why hasn't that seminary dean answered his last letter?

Brandon had told her he'd heard from Dean Swathsmore two months ago.

Dear Brother Fall: We've reviewed your seminary application. We regret to inform you that our scholarship fund is depleted. However, there is the Sattler Fund, scholarships given to those who score high on an essay on a Christian theme. We encourage you to write a paper on a topic relating to the Christian faith and send it as an entry and application for the Sattler Fund. Should you decide to do this, keep in mind, you will not hear from us for several weeks....

Brandon had told her, "I wrote on old Abraham going up Mount Moriah to sacrifice Isaac, and I'm afraid my spirit lost its way...."

How God has led us, now this. How did we get sidetracked from each other last year: Stafford? Maggler?

Lissa was keenly aware that she was indeed thankful that they'd been mature enough to recognize enduring love underneath their hesitancies and ambivalences, and to rise above misjudgments and dead-end trails.

"Yes – God brought us back together." Lissa bowed her head, closed her eyes, and prayed.

* * *

At twelve, an aide entered the room carrying a tray with a bowl of hot chicken soup and a small glass of fruit juice. "We'll try to spoon some of this broth into his mouth. He's got to eat. Can't get better unless he tries to eat."

"Brandon. Brandon." Lissa squeezed his hand.

"Now, Mr. Fall, you got a beautiful lady a sittin right next to you. You ought to open them long lashes and take a peek at her."

His eyes opened. Bewildered at first, they searched, then fell on Lissa's face. "Hello, angel. Why, am I in heaven?" He struggled to smile.

"Darling." Lissa leaned over him to kiss his forehead. "I'm praying. I'm praying, Brandon...." Tears streamed.

"There, there. Don't cry, Lissa. Don't cry. I don't feel the pain at all today. Getting better, you'll see. You'll see."

* * *

Downstairs, a weary Doctor Bowen wrote in his almost illegible handwriting on Brandon's chart: "Symptoms of gangrene. Consult with specialist Harnack when he comes Wednesday."

CHAPTER THIRTY-ONE

They strolled on the open dirt road in front of Brandon's weathered house, Brandon limping, cane in hand, Yippi trotting along in front of them, tongue hanging, face turned lovingly, now and then, toward them.

"Who would of thought one snake could have caused so much trouble, Lissa?" Brandon grinned, feeling the pressure of Lissa's warm palm in his as they strolled. "Tribulations, trouble, more debts, weakened body, yet I recognize the joy of Christ in my being."

Brandon had traces of memory when he hung between life and death in delirium. A bright sweeping light above him, a green and magnified earth in its beauty below, and either the thought, or voices from above saying, "He is near. The Lord is near."

In and out of the delirium, he opened his eyes to glimpse an angel sitting beside his bed, holding his hand, sometimes praying, sometimes smiling. He thought he remembered the angel's soprano voice singing their song. *O perfect love, all human thought transcending....*

"Important thing is, the doctors were able to save your leg, Brandon. The whole community held special prayer services." Lissa stood on her toes, brought his head toward her, and kissed his pale cheek.

"Our wedding, blown right out of the month of April, wasn't it?" Brandon stopped, embraced Lissa, crook of his cane around his arm. He bent and kissed her rosy lips.

"Love triumphs anyway, Brandon. Pastor Elwin had to get busy and do that rush wedding for Amelia Longhorn. Church wedding, too. At her age. Who would have thought it?" Lissa grinned at the news that had given the sewing circle a buzzing new focus for a while.

"And brother Elwin not yet over the shock of Marla Edith's *red wedding*. Brandon grinned. "Wherever there's a pot," he said.

"There's a lid that fits," Lissa chimed in. Their laughter drifted in the summer wind. Lissa noticed that the bee balm was beginning to open, contrasting its lavender blue with the clump of white primroses along the roadside.

"Married Hyde Whitby. Found out Amelia lived and breathed black walnuts. Poor old Hyde, they said he couldn't stop himself from poking down her black walnut pralines." Brandon and Lissa tottered and laughed beneath the shade of the osage orange, feet overshadowed by the primroses.

"Well, I'm glad for Amelia. I know she put herself out for Mother and me the day I got snake-bitten. Doctor had to give her medicine to calm her nerves after she tromped through the woods and over the footbridge that day to her car."

Lissa noticed Brandon wincing. She realized they had walked far enough and must turn around. Thank God, he's getting stronger every day.

"Doctor thinks when my leg heals completely, and if I keep exercising, I may not even have a limp." Brandon turned, placing the most weight on his good leg. "Considerable muscle left in my thigh and calf."

They reviewed their wedding plans for June. Lissa hummed as Brandon sang the words of the song they had focused on with open hearts and souls.

> O perfect Life, be Thou their full assurance
> Of tender charity and steadfast faith....

"It'll be our song always, Lissa. And Lissa, how can I wait to see you in that flowing wedding dress?"

"That's always the groom's task, Brandon. You'll see me soon, veil and all – Mother's roses included. She's so pleased they're heavy with buds and blossoms this year."

"Roses. I always liked roses." Brandon smiled.

"And another thing I almost forgot, Brandon. Aunt Gustie claims she'll have her new teeth by the time of our wedding. Said she's going to lean forward on the front bench and keep grinning at us and break them in real good." This time, Lissa laughed and slapped her thigh, hanging on to Brandon's arm. He clasped her behind her back with his broad hand.

Silence hung as they strolled back toward the weatherbeaten house. Then Brandon asked, doubt reflecting in his voice, "When am I going to hear from that seminary dean about the special scholarship?" Must be my essay didn't pass muster. They must have passed me by."

Then Brandon felt guilty, as though he had neglected a duty, being so poor and not having a typewriter to type his essay.

* * *

Over at Reverend Stafford's house in Branson, Tippy Mae Maggler sloshed her dishrag, helping Marla Edith wash up the mixing bowl and pans from the morning baking. She wiped sweat from her forehead with a swipe of her arm, feed sack dress with ugly red turnip print askew, hiked up in the back. Her red anklets drooped over the tops of runover shoes.

"When we finish this, Tippy Mae, Reverend Stafford wants you to go down to the basement and sort through the onions. Can't let the rotten ones lie there amongst the good ones." Marla Edith smoothed the navy rayon dress over her ample hips, realizing she needed to cut back on the rich foods Reverend Wardley had insisted on. "German chocolate cake. That's what's been doing it," she mumbled to herself.

"Yes, Aunt Marla." Tippy Mae's words hung in the air, lifeless as the banner at the Sinclair Station during dog days.

Anger burned upward like a sour belch. Tippy Mae's mouth unclenched.

"How you expect me to sort them onions an' then hurry over by

JAMES D. YODER

the river to pick them mushrooms the Reverend ordered me to pick today? Huh?" Tippy Mae, hands on her hips, turned to stare at her Aunt Marla Edith, unruffled, wide-eyed, hair sleek in her upsweep which gave her a couple of inches so she would be more compatible with the Reverend's height.

"Your English, Tippy Mae. Your English. No wonder you didn't go to high school. Not only your math." Marla Edith's forehead wrinkled, her mouth puckered. She wondered if that beginning teacher, Lissa Massey, had taught the girl anything at all.

"There'll be time to gather those wild mushrooms, Tippie Mae." Marla Edith continued with the directions for Tippy Mae, "I have my sorority this evening up in Ozark, Tippy Mae. Light dinner served there. Now, since I'm the Reverend's wife, it's all the more appropriate for me not to miss. Around six o'clock, all you have to do is slice those mushrooms, dip them in flour and egg like you see me do chicken breast. Put a little butter in the skillet. When they're golden brown, turn them. Not too hot. Don't burn the Reverned's mushrooms." Marla Edith stared at Tippy Mae to make sure the directions registered.

"Pick them in this heat, then slice them and cook them? Roll them in all that stuff?" Tippy Mae plopped onto a kitchen chair and pouted.

"Now, Tippy Mae, grab your pail. You know we don't want anyone to beat us to those mushrooms. Serve them just as I told you, and I'll bring you some strawberry ice cream from The Palace. How's that?"

Well, Tippy Mae knew that, yes, indeed, Reverend Stafford would be mighty dissappointed if she slouched around and allowed someone else to snatch those wild mushrooms: Eula Botlick, for instance, whose garden backed up to the land where those mushrooms sprouted. Tippy Mae guessed she'd have to be like Topsy in *Uncle Tom's Cabin* and mosey on over there, swinging her pail.

"Afraid of snakes, Aunt Marla Edith, big ole black water moccasins slide up out of the river, hot day like this. Your ex-boyfriend, Brandon Fall, nearly died from that copperhead." Tippy Mae raised her chin, flour smudging her cheek.

176

A BRANSON LOVE

* * *

Tippy Mae stank of the residue of rotting onions smeared on her dress where she'd wiped her palms. She grabbed the chipped granite pail and slouched on down the lane towards the woods at the edge of town. "Mushrooms. Tippie Mae, go fetch the mushrooms. Reverend Stafford dearly loves wild mushrooms," she muttered to herself, kicking gravel and clods with her already damaged shoe toe. Her mind wandered. Old Aunt Marla Edith hightailing it to that uppity sooorrrrrooorrity doings, whatever that is. Too hot in the kitchen to fry mushrooms. Besides, the Reverend barking more commands at her.

Last week, down in that cold, dark cellar – big blacksnake skin hanging on the pipe above her head. Heart nearly stopped beating. Whoooooooeeeee. Let old Marla Edith Mrs. Reverend Wardley Stafffffoooooorrrrrd sashay down 'em stairs, her in her high heels, them big calves hooking a splinter on edges of them steps.

Pent-up resentment escaped like steam from the petcock of the pressure cooker as she muttered and swung her pail.

And that *great* Reverend. Who he think he is? "No, Tippy Mae, that's not the way my wife, Myrna, done it. Potatoes go on the bin along the west wall."

"Well, got news for that Rev-er-endddddd fer sure. Them taters near as rotten as them onions I smeared around in just this morning." Her mutterings were swept away in the wind.

A flop-eared hound loped up behind her, got a sniff of her onion dress and hightailed it around and on down the road.

"Now where they say them mushrooms are? Behind old lady Bottlelicker, whatever they say her name is; behind her garden? Where's that? Sun's hot – scalding my scalp." The discordant mumblings scattered in the hot air.

Tippy Mae, feeling sorry for herself, remembered last year's social studies in Miss Massey's school about those medieval times, how the kings and queens took advantage of kitchen girls. Scullery maids, that's what they called them. "Well, I got news for Mr. and Mrs. Reverrrrr-enddddd. I ain't no scullery maid." The stray dog turned at her mumblings. "Besides, I ain't gonna eat any of the

Reverend's ole mushrooms. I'll be too hot, cooking 'em over that woodstove, and I'm jes' too mad at him."

* * *

It hadn't been so bad after all, filling the blue-granite bucket. Lots of 'em. Little white-capped whatever-their-names were. Tippy Mae forgot. With a breeze to her back, the trip home was considerable easier, though she had to shift the bucket from arm to arm.

"I guess old Aunt Biddie Marla Edith and her Rever-enddddd'll be mighty pleased after all. Ought to give me a quarter, being's I got there before that old Botlicker woman." Only thing, Tippy Mae decided it would be best if she didn't tell the Mr. and Mrs. Stafford that she didn't actually have to walk *all* the way down to behind that old lady's garden. Lots of mushrooms popping up on the left side of the road, half-way down. Yes, Tippy Mae concluded. "The Lord, he does provide."

CHAPTER THIRTY-TWO

Over at the Massey farm, Slade, finished with hoeing the cabbages in the garden, sat in the porch swing, reading his Buck Rogers *Little Big Book* which cost him a dime down at Vern's Five-and-Dime in Branson.

Soon-to-be married big sister was upstairs stitching away at that veil on the Singer sewing machine. Slade worried when he thought of the upcoming wedding. They wanted him to take part. What could he do? Caught between childhood and adolescence at age eleven? He hoped they'd forget about him with all the other details.

The telephone gave a nerve-wracking jangle, two short rings, two long. Their number: six on line two.

"Slade, that the phone? Would you mind answering it? My hands are all covered with dough," Estra called from the kitchen.

"Yes, Mother. I'll get it." The swing caught in the wind as he rolled off the slatted boards and padded barefooted through the dining room door and over to the wall telephone by the burled-walnut secretary. Slade felt some comfort. At least we still have a telephone, even though the radio batteries are dead. "Hello, Massey's." Slade leaned against the side of the secretary in his striped overalls, one hand digging in a pocket, feeling for his penknife as he listened to a frenzied voice on the line.

"Miss Amelia? Yes. Yes, oh, Reverend Stafford sick? In the hospital at Ozark? Here, Miss Amelia, I'd better let you talk to my mother.

"Mom, something about Reverend Stafford. Taken real sick and might die. Over at the Mercy Hospital in Ozark. You'd better come and talk with Amelia."

Estra dried her hands on the roller towel by the wash basin and hurried to the phone as she brushed a strand of hair back from her forehead.

"Hello, Amelia. Slade mentioned Elder Stafford–"

"Oh, Estra," echoed the voice through the receiver. "You won't believe this. Marla Edith Stafford had to call the ambulance last night. Terrible. Just terrible. Why, I remember not too long ago cooking a fine dinner for the Reverend when he was at my house...." Amelia's voice failed her as she broke into tears.

"Amelia? Can you talk, Amelia? What happened?" Estra's hand now over her heart.

"Yes, Estra. Oh, it is just a calamity. You know that Tippy Mae Maggler girl, one never went on to high school, well, she is careless, isn't she? Seems like they sent her out to pick some wild mushrooms and bring them in for Reverend Stafford. Oh, Estra. I guess the poor man is suffering most pitiful and may die." Amelia's voice choked.

Oh, dear Jesus, Estra thought. Banks closing, men out of work, people starving and homeless, Brandon sidetracked by that deceiving man, Marla Edith's claws, that terrible copperhead bite, now this. Oh my, oh my. Lord. Lord.

"Why, Amelia. I am so very sorry to hear that. Why, what did you say he ate? Mushrooms? Well, isn't it late in the spring for the morels? Why, they usually come up in April under the dead elm trees, don't they?"

"Well, Estra, that ignorant girl picked the wrong ones. I heard that Tippy Mae said they was the sweetest-smelling mushrooms that they ever smelled when they were sizzling in the pan."

Estra decided after she hung up to call over at old Preacher Supple's house and ask them to get a prayer circle started for Reverend Stafford. Pompous? Made grievous mistakes? Yes. But our Christian duty to forgive. Thoughts layered in her mind. What the poor man must be going through. Bet they pumped his stomach. Estra whispered a prayer: "Lord, reach out your hand...."

*   *   *

Brandon stopped at his mailbox at the end of the lane, reached into the rusty cavern for the mail: the *Gazette*, a flier from The Valentine Theater in Ozark, Shirley Temple's smiling face covering one-third of the page.

He was glad Lissa had driven over right away in her Mother's Model A. Right thing to do, even though Lissa was fussing about the way she looked. They rattled across Dodie Creek Bridge in Brandon's gunmetal-colored Ford. Lissa rolled up her window to keep out the dust.

Brandon thought Lissa was stunning, those wisps of blond hair straying a little, and that pale yellow frock.

"Hurry, Brandon. We must try to get there before he...." Lissa didn't finish the sentence.

Brandon looked over at her and noticed her forehead was creased, her eyes reflecting pain as she thought of powerful Stafford, prostrate in a hospital bed, near death. "Dear Lord, let them tend him before the poison...."

"Think they'll be hard on Tippy Mae over this, Lissa?" Brandon guided the Ford around a brown terrapin that had crawled out into the track.

"Tippy Mae is a good girl. A good girl, Brandon. She knows a lot more than people give her credit for. I hope they don't blame her. I expect she gets more orders at that house with both Stafford and Marla Edith than a Baldknobber gang could carry out. Oh, poor, poor Tippy Mae. We'll have to make sure to see her and comfort her."

"Well, if you ask me, Lissa, her pa and ma are partly to blame, not sending her on to high school. That's where she belongs. Not cooking maid for the Staffords." He thumped the hard steering wheel with the butt of one hand.

"Yes, I'd about decided to do something myself, Brandon. After this is over, I plan to discuss it with her parents. Even with Marla Edith if I have to. Marla Edith's partially responsible, too, I believe."

The clock in the court house tower indicated four o'clock as Brandon guided the Ford into one of the three parking spaces in the lot to the left of the yellow brick hospital looming before them, paint cracking on the wooden trim.

Neither Brandon nor Lissa liked the carbolic acid and lysol smell of hospitals. Starched-capped, white-uniformed nurses with long faces hurried down the wooden plank aisles. The summer heat already bore down, but the wide, tall windows, thrust open, allowed blessed relief from a breeze.

"Room seventeen on second," said the rosy-cheeked Grey Lady at the front desk; she wore her long-sleeved pink-cuffed uniform in spite of the heat.

The wide, wooden stairs creaked and groaned as they climbed. Oh, Lord, let him live. He's a good man, down underneath, he has his problems, but.... Brandon limped as he strained on the steps.

Marla Edith, who evidently had taken some time to dress for the occasion before the ambulance arrived at the parsonage, sat in the mock-leather chair by the high iron bed where the stricken man lay, wide-chested, face white as the sheet covering him, salt-and-pepper spread of hair shoved up by the pillow.

Lissa glanced at Marla Edith. Look how Marla Edith's dressed. Silk dress, black-toned silk hose and patent pumps, heels at least three inches. Pink nail polish. Pearls? Bet those belonged to Myrna.... Lissa checked her thoughts as they entered the room.

"Oh, Miss Massey, Miss Massey." Tippy Mae crept away from the doorsill that held her up. The girl's tear-streaked, terror-ridden face told the full story. "I didn't mean to, Miss Massey. You all have to tell them. I didn't mean to. Mushrooms poppin' up everywhere. Could a walked further, but 'em mushrooms sure was pretty, Miss Massey, and you ought to a been there to smell them frying—"

"Be quiet, Tippy Mae. Be quiet. I've heard enough of your whimpering. Why, Brandon. Lissa. Good of you to come. Yes." Marla Edith leaned forward, pearls swinging, her face reflecting both her concern and her realization that this was a time and place to still announce who she was, and to whom they were speaking. She shifted a silk-sheathed calf back behind another.

"How is Reverend Stafford?" Brandon and Lissa whispered together, Lissa reaching out to brush Marla Edith's hand.

"Oh, it was just terrible. Terrible. I couldn't begin to tell you...."

Tears crept to the corners of Marla Edith's wide, round eyes. She shifted and dabbed her eyes, the heady odor of her Bridal Night perfume rising from the tiny laced-linen handkerchief.

"We are all praying, Marla Edith. All praying." Brandon lifted a brown brogue in his discomfort before Marla Edith. Would the stricken churchman recover?

"Doctor expects him to recover? Got to the hospital in time, didn't you, Marla Edith?" Lissa asked the question on Brandon's mind.

"We don't know yet. Don't know.... Oh, Lissa, oh, Brandon, my heart, such a sorrow." Marla Edith allowed herself a heaving sob, open black eyes pleading for their pity.

Considering his last meeting with Marla Edith by Slavanskie's Produce in Trumpet, Brandon wondered whether or not he should offer to pray. He had snatched up his worn Bible before he left home.

"Brother Brandon, I-I'd be pleased, and believe the Reverend would be very pleased if you'd offer a prayer. Yes. A prayer." Marla Edith wiped her eyes again, lifted her chin, reached out to place her hand on top of her husband's heavy-veined ones, folded on his chest. "Yes, Brother Brandon, do pray for him." The diamond in the ring on her finger sparkled in the sunlight from the open window.

* * *

On their way out of the hospital, a bald-headed doctor in a crumpled white coat, who looked as if he'd been working for forty-eight hours straight without rest, leaned over, handing Nurse Stenton the chart.

"These country folks. One would have thought educated people like Stafford and Marla Edith would have had more caution. Can't blame a child for this. Pity the child. She's the one have trouble living it down. Ever hear of such a name, Violet? Tippy Mae?"

"No, Doctor Hammers, I never in all my days heard of such a name. Tippy Mae." Nurse Violet took the chart. "What kind of toadstools did he eat, Doctor Hammers? Were you able to find out?"

"Had to look it up in the encyclopedia. This time of the year lots of toadstools pushing up. Guess that schoolteacher, Marla Edith, or

Mrs. Stafford, now, thought they were the edible *Amanitas. Amanita Crocea*, actual name. Had three other cases like this last year." Doctor Hammers cleared his throat, loosening his blue tie.

"Instead that girl got ahold of something called *Destroying Angel*. It's an Amanita mushroom too. Hard to tell the difference. I doubt if the Reverend's wife, what's her name? Marla Edith, would have been able to tell the difference. Tragic. Tragic."

* * *

"Wait. Wait, Miss Massey. Wait for me. Aunt Marla Edith wanted me to ask you if you could drive me past the parsonage in Branson. I'm surely glad to get out of that room. Oh, Miss Massey, you just ought to have seen the green vomit.... I never saw such heaves. Poor, poor Reverend Stafford, an' me sometimes thinking mean things about him and Aunt Marla Edith. I'll probably go straight to hell."

"Oh, Tippy Mae. Don't say such a thing. It was a mistake. We all make mistakes. Reverend Stafford himself, when he looked at the mushrooms, should have said something if they didn't look right. No. Tippy Mae, God loves you. I love you. Come here."

Lissa, realizing the sweating, overweight girl with the greasy hair swept back behind her stick-out ears needed comfort, brought Tippy Mae to her bosom. "There, Tiphanie Mae." Lissa's warm hands caressed the sobbing girl's back.

"Oh, Miss Massey, you about the only one knows my real name. I get so tired of everyone yellin 'Here, Tippy Mae; there, Tippy Mae,' just like they calling a dog." She sobbed.

"There, there, Tiphanie Mae. We'll drive you on home, and I'll stay with you until your aunt Marla Edith gets back from the hospital. There, there." Tears flowed down Lissa's cheeks at the broken-hearted girl's plight.

Lissa resolved right there: tomorrow. Tomorrow we're going to talk about this girl's future.

CHAPTER THIRTY-THREE

Two days later, when Marla Edith Maggler called from Mercy Hospital up in Ozark, Lissa, who answered the phone, noticed the change in Marla Edith's voice.
"Lissa, I know Brandon doesn't have a telephone. Could you please drive over and tell him that Reverend Stafford wants to see him? You too, Lissa, the two of you."
"Why, yes, Marla Edith. Yes. And how is Reverend Stafford doing, better, I hope?"
Lissa noticed a calmer tone in Marla Edith's voice, less demanding, less grating, less as though she was struggling with a tumbleweed rolling across her garden.
"Yes. Thank God, Lissa. Thank God. Wardley's much better. He's sitting up now and had a little milk and oatmeal for breakfast. Doctor Hammers believes he'll be coming home by the end of the week. Thank God."
Something had happened to Marla Edith. The pain, the suffering, and the shock. Could it be that God had worked through all her wrestlings, jealousies, and pushings?

* * *

Closing his mailbox, lifting his eyes from the three pieces of mail, Brandon smiled, seeing Lissa drive up the road toward his place. Only twenty-five more days. Mock orange would be blooming.

Nothing sweeter in a church than baskets of mock orange, white, like his bride's dress.

Brandon noticed an ivory-colored envelope addressed to him. When Lissa parked her Ford by the mimosa tree, he decided to lay the mail on the table in the kitchen so as to not keep Lissa waiting.

"Brandon, Reverend Stafford wants to see us. Marla Edith called and requested that we come to the hospital."

"Well. Stafford wants to see us? Asked for us?" A part of Brandon's mind didn't want to believe it, that a man who, in his pomposity and self-serving connivings, slammed the door on his ministry at White Oak Church, now actually called for his presence. And after that discussion, or confrontation, in his office down in Reeds Spring where I compared him to Baalam?

* * *

Brandon's Model A lurched toward Ozark, down the vale past the two rows of pines and up the clay hill as blackbirds swirled in the sky. White clouds billowed against the blue expanse above them. A stiff breeze, whipping over Iron Mountain, hit the windshield.

He's so silent today, thought Lissa, hands folded in the lap of her box-pleated tan skirt. He does look like Abraham Lincoln when that heavy lock falls down over his forehead and he stares straight ahead.

Brandon drove in silence as if his mind whirled with questions. He'd rejected moving in, after the wedding, with either Estra or his parents. If the drought continued another year, they couldn't earn enough on the forty to pay rent in Branson, even on a very small cottage. His forehead creased.

Lissa, seeing his face, reached over and touched his hand on the wooden wheel. "I haven't signed my school contract yet, Brandon, but I will turn it in before the end of the month. We'll have income. Doors will open. You'll see. 'Faith produces hope. Hope produces endurance.' St. Paul."

Marla Edith rose to meet them as they approached Wardley Stafford's hospital room. Lissa noticed Marla Edith's more sedate poise. Even though it was summer, she strode forward in two-inch heel pumps, navy rayon dress with long sleeves and a high collar.

Her hair was swept up and pinned in a French roll. She wore no jewelery and no lipstick today.

"I'm glad to see you, Lissa. Brandon." Marla Edith extended her hand. "Reverend Stafford's waiting for you. He said it was very important."

"Why, Lissa. Why, Brandon. Yes. Yes." The powerful man, subdued by his ordeal, raised himself against his pillow, arms encased in pearl-grey rayon pajamas. He extended his large hand.

"Hello, Brother Stafford. I'm so glad you're better." Brandon clasped the offered hand, noticing the warmth.

"And the bride-to-be. Soon be Mrs. Brandon Fall, won't you?" Wardley offered Lissa his hand next.

"Why, yes. In June, Brother Stafford. I, too, am so glad you're better. We all have been praying for you."

"I had chairs brought in for you. Please sit down." Marla Edith pointed toward the two straight chairs facing the bed and her husband.

"Yes. God brought me through. I believe it. Prayers of the church. Yes, well, I've had opportunity to think about some things and decided I needed to tell you something, Brandon. And Lissa, it affected my relationship with you, also."

What could it be? Had he listened to the angel in the path? Brandon's eyes focused intensely on Wardley Stafford's face. He swallowed, Adam's apple bobbing. Lissa reached over to clasp Brandon's arm. What could it be?

"Brandon, start with you. I called you here today to make a confession. Yes, a confession."

Brandon's eyes opened wider. Lissa's hand tightened on his arm.

Tears appeared at the corners of Wardley's eyes. "I want to confess to you, Brandon, that I was the one responsible for you being set aside that day at White Oak Church." He cleared his throat. Marla Edith leaned over and gently patted his left hand on his breast.

"Something happened when I was a hard-working student in seminary, many years ago. So long ago. I tried to bury it. Tried not think about it. Almost convinced myself that I had forgotten about it." Stafford turned his handsome head to look at a cardinal that perched on the window sill outside.

Then he turned back. "I was dishonest on an important examination in Church History. I made a weak attempt to straighten it out but failed. As a result of my dishonesty, I ended by being valedictorian of the seminary graduating class. My dishonesty shoved aside Rhutley Rennart's brother, Enis, who was in seminary at the same time. Without my cheating, Enis would probably have been the valedictorian. The Rennarts knew about it and didn't forget it. Resentment burned through the years, and I understand it."

The words hung in the air, circling like the oak blades of the old ceiling fan in the cavernous waiting room downstairs. How could it be, a powerful clergyman like Wardley, once cheating on an exam? Lissa's hand crept to her chin.

"Deacon Rennart pressured me. Actually blackmailed me. He said he'd go to the church board and conference head about it if I didn't halt your ordination and endorse his son-in-law, Elwin Nevins, a seminary graduate."

Wardley reached out for Marla Edith's hand, gripped it, smiled at her with affection, then turned back to Brandon and Lissa.

Tears glistened in the churchman's granite eyes. "I want to ask you to forgive me, Brandon. Forgive my sin. You too, Lissa. You knew something deeper was going on, and I just couldn't face it. Pride. Pride. The sin of pride."

The silence hung. Lissa looked at Brandon's deep brown eyes, wide in surprise at the revelation.

"I was very angry at you, Brandon, that you had the gumption to drive all the way over to Reeds Spring to confront me. Balaam and his ass and the angel." Wardley smiled, looking with fondness at the young couple, who were reeling from the confession.

"Give you a lot of credit for that, Brandon Fall. Yes. Make a fine, fine minister. You have determination and courage. And you can speak the truth. Strange, though I resented it very much, what you said to me caused my admiration for you to grow."

Wardley glanced out the window where the tops of the dogwood trees nodded in the westerly breeze. Earth and sky reflected cleanliness and sweetness. He turned back.

"Can you find it in your hearts to forgive me, Brandon? Lissa?" He waited, trace of a smile at his lips.

A BRANSON LOVE

Brandon reached for Elder Stafford's hand. "Yes, Brother Stafford. Yes. I forgive you. I so very much appreciate that you've cleared it up. Now I can let go of my own bitterness. I've prayed about it, but parts of it still hung on. Yes, I forgive you and let it go." Brandon stood still clasping the minister's hand.

Wardley looked over at Lissa, who rose to stand beside her fiance.

"Can you find it in your heart to forgive me, Lissa?"

"Yes. I forgive you. I knew something troubled you deeply. Something you couldn't talk about in full honesty. Yes, thank you for clearing it up." Lissa reached for Brandon's arm.

Marla Edith twisted on her chair. Her hand swept up to check her French roll. She cleared her throat, her eyelids batting a Betty Boop's bat. "Why, uh – Lissa, there is something – uh...."

Lissa, turning her wondering face, waited.

"Uh, Lissa, I ought to say something too. Yes. Why – uh – I blamed you for the Blue Vale School situation – having to mud it all the way over to Dodder School for a job, two years ago." Marla Edith lifted her head, her breast heaved.

"Why, Marla Edith, yes, well, I-I never quite understood–"

"I ought not to have blamed you like I did, telling folks that you *stole* my school. I admit I was foolish going out on that dance floor with Melvin Pempton." Her dimpled fist brushed her lips as she cleared her throat. "Teacher in these parts ought not to try the Charlston like I did that night. And the place, well–"

Lissa reached forth a hand, touching Marla Edith's. "I can understand how hurt you could be over losing your schoolteaching job, Marla Edith. Especially in times like these. And I struggled about whether or not to sign that contract. But with one of the deacons insisting, and Papa dying, why, I–"

"You did the right thing. I wouldn't have hesitated one minute, Lissa." Marla's lips spread into a wide smile. "Not a minute. And things turned out quite well for me." Here Marla lifted her head into its usual surveying position, patted her hair again in back, her other hand resting on Reverend Stafford's. "I want your forgiveness, Lissa. I ought to have behaved with more grace. I knew better, but it was the anger, you know. The Maggler anger." Her head lowered.

JAMES D. YODER

"Marla Edith, you're forgiven. It was hard for me, teaching at Blue Vale, considering the circumstances. And I do understand how confused and hurt you must have felt, and how you may have blamed yourself. Yes, Marla Edith, I can forgive you." Lissa patted Marla's hand.

"You deserved the trophy last Activity Day up at Ozark, too, Lissa. Your students earned it," Marla Edith added.

"Forgive me for the way I behaved that day, too, Marla Edith. I gloated. I was determined to beat you and your school. My attitude was very wrong. We won the trophy, but I felt guilty about it."

Marla Edith smiled. "Think no more of it, Lissa. I goaded you that day. Snubbed you, too, so we were even. You're forgiven, Lissa." She held Lissa's hand for a moment.

Lissa glanced over at Brandon, wondering if it was time to ease out of the room and let Reverend Stafford sleep.

"Another thing." Marla Edith's black eyes cut over to Brandon, who was straightening his thin necktie. "Brandon, I, er – I shouldn't have delayed so in sending Cousin Moody that Bible School money. Neglect like that was wrong of me."

Brandon, startled, eyelids lifting, dragged his hands out of his pockets. "Well, yes, uh – perhaps you are right about that, Marla Edith. But I should have sent the money on the very next day. I was the superintendent. I did, though, expect you to follow through as you said you would."

"Right, Brandon. You're right." Marla Edith shifted one thigh over another. "Real slouchy of me to be so careless in bookkeeping. It was my Maggler anger that made me go to Deacon Whitsitt about it. I did shove that loan off on you that day. You, compromised without a car. Can you forgive me?"

"I can, Marla Edith. Let's let it drop. It's all cleared up, now. I really do believe that verse that says, 'All things work together for–'"

"No more. Say no more." Marla stood, head thrown back, schoolmom look on her face. "Let's shake, Brandon. Water's under the bridge." She grinned.

Brandon stretched out a big, tanned hand, which enveloped her olive-toned one. "Water's under the bridge." He smiled.

"And," Marla Edith said, "before you go, I want to thank you for taking Tiphanie Mae back home two days ago and staying with her, Lissa."

"You're welcome, Marla Edith." Lissa wanted to say more about Tiphanie Mae but wondered if this was the time.

"I-I must say something else." Marla Edith rose, her eyes steady and looking straight at Lissa's face.

"I've concluded, along with my husband, that the arrangement with Tiphanie Mae isn't the best for her. She must get to high school. Reverend Stafford and I have decided to pay Ruthanne Nolton, one of the Branson high-school teachers, to tutor Tiphanie Mae in English and math for the rest of the summer. I personally plan to take her down to the school in the fall and enroll her."

"Why, Marla Edith." Lissa reached for her hand. "I've been thinking of it, too, Tiphanie Mae's schooling. Yes, actually she is very bright, just needs love and encouragement."

"And Lissa, you have good judgment when it comes to colors and clothing. Wardley and I want you to take this twenty-dollar bill and stop at Regent's Dress Shop on the square in Ozark and buy Tiphanie Mae some new clothes – dress, blouse, and skirt. You pick them out for her." Marla Edith smiled as if the jealousies and hateful attitudes of yesterday had seeped beneath a log in the woods.

Lissa could scarcely believe it, but she took the bill. "Thank you, Marla Edith. We'll stop today, won't we, Brandon? How very kind of you. And I just might add five dollars of my own."

* * *

When they had driven past the pines and down the clay hill, Brandon took the loop that meandered down Main Street in Branson. Lissa glanced back at the packages on the back seat containing a yellow dress, two skirts, and a blouse for Tippy Mae.

"My, look at that. Brick's Notions closed, wind blowing leaves in the doorway. What next in these times?" asked Brandon.

"Stop. Pull over to the curb, Brandon. There comes Aunt Gustie out of Vilus Litlock's dental office."

There stood Aunt Gustie holding one of those blue cotton

handkerchiefs the farmers use over her mouth. She headed for Silas Whitsitt's truck parked at the curb.

"Aunt Gustie. Aunt Gustie." Lissa waved. "Over here, Aunt Gustie."

Then the old woman in the long calico dress and high-topped shoes noticed them. She stopped and stared, handkerchief still over her lower face.

"Would you like a lift on home to your place, Aunt Gustie?" Brandon called out.

The old woman stood and continued to stare, wind whipping the calico about her thighs. Then her hand slid away from her mouth and bony chin. She was about to speak.

"New teeth, Brandon, Aunt Gustie's come in for her new teeth." Lissa squeezed Brandon's arm, waiting.

Gustie's lips cracked and trembled.

With fear in her eyes, her thin lips parted and kept on parting into a wide grin. Her new store teeth gleamed like hewn granite stones in the lower row on the east side of the Citizen's Bank. Large, even. Set in a row.

"Got my new teeth." Gustie stood her ground. Unmovable. Then she added, "Do I look horsey?" Gustie's glittering white, oversized teeth clacked and clattered in their unfamiliarity of tangling with tongue and words.

Lissa stifled a laugh. Brandon gasped. Horsey, they thought together as they stared at each other, trying not to laugh.

"Why, Aunt Gustie, white teeth like that, you're going to give St. Peter quite a smile, some day," said Brandon, trying to avoid the "horsey" question.

"Yes, Aunt Gustie. White. Really white. Now you can sit on the front row at our wedding. White mock orange and roses. White dresses, and you'll fit right in with your new white teeth." What else could she say?

"No." Aunt Gustie announced, "I'll get home same way I come, in Silas Whitsitt's truck. Give these teeth a try at that rough ride, see if they stay in place. Ain't gonna stay put, hafta take 'em back to Vilus."

Brandon stopped the Model A under the spreading hackberry at the edge of town so that they could release the laughter. Lissa cried in joy and in pity, knowing that she could never say another word about the splendid new teeth of her favorite aunt. "And Brandon, we'll have to stop picking apples from that horse apple tree for a while."

Brandon turned the car up the slope toward their weathered home, smoke gently rising in the air from Serena's kitchen range.

Then Brandon remembered the letter in the ivory envelope. Almost forgot. "Come on in, Lissa. I want to check the mail again. I was in a hurry to get over to the hospital and I didn't take time to open the letter that came this morning."

"Why, Lissa, come on in. Take the split-willow-rocker there." Serena beamed, one hand in her starched apron pocket. "I've been thinking, Lissa, if you'd want a basket of my mock orange for the church, day of your wedding?"

"Why, Serena, that'd be just fine, I do love mock orange." She lifted the bough of trumpet vine she'd snatched by the gate post, the three blossoms stretching outwards to her nose. "Serena, I always did love trumpet vine, too."

"Lissa. Lissa. Come here."

But Brandon didn't wait for Lissa to come to him. He marched right into the middle of the braided rug on the floor of the living room. "Lissa, Mother, Pa. Listen to this." His big hands trembled as they held the ivory page.

Dear Brother Fall:

We regret that it took so long to reply to your entry in the Sattler essay scholarship plan. I am happy to inform you that the judges selected your essay on **Abraham and Moriah** *for first place. This means that if you care to accept it, you will have a full seminary scholarship. You will have thirty days wherein you may make your decision.*

We do want to encourage you, especially in these hard times, to accept this fine offer. We would very much like to have a scholar with your ability in our seminary. I can also tell you that only yesterday, we received a fine letter of recommendation from a bishop in your denomination, Reverend Wardley Stafford. I'm sure you know him....

"Bless God. Bless God." Serena rushed over to embrace her astonished son.

It seemed like all of the June sunshine flooded the room and their hearts in one loving burst. "Oh, Brandon. Brandon. Yes. Yes. I've never forgotten your sermon that day over at the church."

"What was it, Lissa?" Brandon's eyes widened.

"Why, darling, you told us all from that passage from St. Paul. 'Rejoice always ... the Lord is at hand.' I've never ceased to believe it, Brandon."

Lissa walked over, placed her arms around his neck, her hand raking through the curly hair she so loved.

She raised the trumpet vine bough to his face. "Listen, Brandon. Listen and you can hear what those little orange trumpets are playing."

Brandon leaned down to listen. "Lissa, I can't hear...."

"Yes, Brandon, yes. Listen carefully, they're trumpeting: "Guess Mrs. Lissa Fall will be teaching in Kansas City, come autumn."

"Why, yes, Lissa, that's what they're trumpeting."

THE END